SERIAL KILLER

SERIAL KILLER

JUDGE, JURY, & EXECUTIONER™ BOOK THREE

CRAIG MARTELLE
MICHAEL ANDERLE

LMBPN Publishing
PMB 196, 2540 South Maryland Pkwy
Las Vegas, NV 89109

First US edition, September 2018
Print ISBN: 978-1-64202-466-1

SERIAL KILLER TEAM

Thanks to our Beta Readers

Micky Cocker
James Caplan
Kelly O'Donnell

Thanks to the JIT Readers

Mary Morris
John Ashmore
James Caplan
Peter Manis
Daniel Weigert
Keith Verret
Kelly O'Donnell
Paul Westman
Kelly Bowerman

If I've missed anyone, please let me know!

Editor
Lynne Stiegler

We can't write without those who support us
On the home front, we thank you for being there for us

We wouldn't be able to do this for a living if it weren't for our readers
We thank you for reading our books

CHAPTER ONE

The diplomat bowed to the welcoming committee. Her delegation stood at a respectful distance. "Thank you for your invitation to Collum," she said pleasantly.

The male, a representative from the Chancellor's office, smiled broadly. "We could not be more pleased with the arrival of the females from Zaxxon."

Her pleasant demeanor evaporated. "There are no males on my planet," she replied coldly. "We are what we are. No need to caveat our existence."

"My apologies, Ambassador." The man bowed deeply to show his sincerity.

The Zaxxon jerked unnaturally before glancing at the hole in her chest. She looked up, confusion and surprise wrestling to dominate her expression, and started to topple. No one moved until she hit the ground, already dead.

No one had heard a shot or realized the ambassador had been murdered until after the killer had escaped.

"Training for a couple weeks before we accept new missions," Grainger told the Magistrates. Jael, Chi, Buster, and Rivka nodded intermittently as he looked from face to face.

"Two things. They're called 'cases,' and give me time to get my crew into the Pod-doc for an upgrade or two," Rivka stated, raising one eyebrow in Grainger's direction.

He threw his hands up. "What?"

"Maybe a case where we're not fighting a war?" Rivka asked. "I'm a lawyer first. Your galaxy-jarring missions call for a heavier hand." She held hers out to show they were small and delicate. Cheese Blintz and Bustamove put their hands next to hers, showing that theirs were bigger.

"Nope." He crossed his arms and leaned back, a smug look on his face.

"I only deal with royalty," Chi stated, smiling.

"I don't do guns," Jael offered.

Buster didn't say anything until all eyes turned toward him. "Fine. Now that Philko ascended to being an AI, I find myself strangely intrigued by cybercrime."

"*White Collar Crime*, a new weekly series starring Bustamove," Grainger said in his best announcer's voice.

"I knew I shouldn't have said anything."

"You'll never see another cybercrime," Rivka told him, mimicking Grainger. "What case do you want? That's nice. NO! You get something completely different." She looked pointedly at the Magistrate at the head of the table.

Grainger shrugged. "As long as we keep winning, we're not changing the playbook. Ain't no I in Team.

What do you say we order some pizzas, throw the iron around, and then hop on my ship for a quick ride to Opheramin?"

"I'm sorry, I must have drifted off from the mind-numbing drone of your voice." Jael leaned forward and locked eyes with Grainger. "I thought you said we were leaving the station?"

"That's exactly what we're going to do."

"Why?" Chi asked.

"Because maybe you don't get to know what we're doing for training. This is important, and once it's over, you'll see why. Did no one hear the part about pizza?"

"I like a good pizza. Are you buying?" Buster asked.

"Red is going to want to go," Rivka stated flatly, "especially if there's pizza."

"Pizza first, then go."

"So we're taking pizza with us in our space suits?" Jael asked.

Grainger stood, grabbed his datapad and strolled away, nose high in the air. He refused to engage further at this juvenile level, or rather at the legal intern level where everything was questioned.

He smiled as the others followed him out.

***

After the workout that didn't include sparring because Grainger didn't have enough time to send someone to the Pod-doc, they cleaned up and reconvened at one of the many airlocks. Grainger had pre-staged a number of spacesuits.

Red and Lindy were waiting. "How did you find out?" Grainger wondered, confusion holding him hostage.

"What kind of bodyguard would I be if I didn't know where my charge was?" Red crossed his arms and looked down at the Magistrate.

"And I'm with him. She's our responsibility. If she leaves the station, so do we." Lindy mirrored Red's pose.

"There won't be any danger," Grainger stated weakly before conceding. "Suit up. You won't need any of your gear."

Red removed one strap and then the other to set his unusually long backpack on the deck. "I always need my gear," he remarked, opening the top to reveal two railguns, a shotgun, grenades, and an assortment of items illegal outside of the military. Lindy smiled and wiggled her eyebrows. He secured it again and loosened the straps so it would fit around a bulky environmental suit.

"Suit up! We got places to go and people to see." Grainger pumped one fist, the military signal for hurry up.

Rivka gripped her bodyguards' arms and mouthed, "Thank you."

"Hang on," Chi declared. He opened his datapad. "Lexi, if you would be so kind, please have twenty large pizzas with a variety of toppings delivered flash-frozen to the airlock on Level Four. Tell All Guns Blazing to charge them to Grainger's account."

"I'll need Grainger's verbal confirmation. Certain Magistrates have been charging a great deal to his account without his authorization. Those charges have been removed from the appropriate people's future pay."

"Go ahead, Lexi," Grainger said, his gaze fixed on something inside his suit.

"This is how you wanted us to find out that you docked our pay?"

"You spent the money, you pay the piper," Grainger retorted, looking from one scowling face to the next until he got to Red and Lindy. They both shrugged.

"I charge things to *her* account," Red admitted, pointing at Rivka with his thumb.

"Do we want to argue about money? Are we so motivated by credits that common decency and self-discipline disappears? I'm embarrassed!" Grainger shook his finger at the Magistrates.

"I have to agree with my learned colleague," Buster added. "What are we if our words can't be believed?"

"Are you being audited or something?" Jael asked as Grainger stood sharply in the spotlight of the Magistrates' withering stares.

"Hang on!" Grainger held up his hands to create a physical barrier. "Yes. I'm being audited, but I'm sure it'll be fine. Magistrates have to be aboveboard on everything. How can we mete out Justice if we are above the law? Keep your noses clean, and point well taken. I promised pizzas, and you know what? I'm prepared to eat my body weight in pies and beer. I like beer with my pie."

Rivka opened her mouth to deliver a witty retort and decided against it. He was still her boss, in an odd way, and she respected that. "I'm not going to be last," Rivka said instead. She hurried to finish dressing. AGB's efficiency meant that the pizzas were delivered minutes after the last person was ready.

"Red, can you take these?" Grainger asked.

Vered shook his head. "Sorry, Magistrate, but I'm on the clock. I have to have my hands free in case something needs killing. And so does she, before you ask." Lindy nodded.

Chi faced Buster, and they started pounding on each other's shoulders. They hooted and cheered before reaching for the stack of pies. The delivery bot turned without a sound and flew away.

"What the hell was that about?" Jael asked.

"Sometimes, even though you know something is right, you still have to psych yourself up to do it," Bustamove told her.

"I don't have anything to say to that. Status check?" Grainger called.

The other six people in the airlock called green. "I'm green, too. Cycling the airlock." He punched the button and the air was sucked into a storage tank, replaced by the near vacuum of space. The outer hatch popped and slowly opened. Grainger led the way into space, activating the pneumatic jets on his boots to propel him head-first.

The others followed. Chi and Buster somersaulted and rolled, all the while maintaining a firm grip on the pizzas.

Grainger headed toward the upper section of the space station. The loose group followed. Lindy and Red flanked Rivka. Each carried one of the rail guns, with the trigger guard released so their gloved fingers fit inside to pull the trigger. The Magistrate couldn't tell if the others were uncomfortable with the armed escort, but Rivka felt more at ease.

Whether for status or peace of mind, she had to admit that she liked having bodyguards.

When Grainger reached an odd projection on Federation Border Station 7, he signaled for the group to gather around.

He activated the comm system for the suits. "What do you think we have here?"

Rivka expected some sort of trick, but turned to examine the outcropping. The metal was a different color from that of the main station, and the welds weren't standard.

Buster and Chi moved as close as they could, but the pizzas hindered a close-up inspection. Jael took the lead in classifying the projection. "Added on after initial construction. It's not labeled for use and safety as it should be. What does it do?"

Rivka finished her circumnavigation of the small attachment before consulting with Red. When she finished she slid across the surface, activating her magnetic boots to stop her so she could stand on it.

The others turned their eyes to her. "You have something, Zombie?"

"It's a deactivated bomb with the explosives removed, I expect."

"What the hell are you playing at?" Chi exclaimed, backpedaling away from the projection. Buster was more deliberate in his departure, activating his jets to propel him past his fellow Magistrate.

"Since we have to be all things, it's about seeing what may be right in front of us, but with different eyes. When there's a crime, we collect the evidence. Many times we can stop future crime by prosecuting those responsible for past illegal activities. The more times someone gets away with their crimes, the bolder they become.

"Although a bomb on the outside of a station may be a military issue, this one came to us when it was determined that it was a commercial construct developed by an individual to further his empire. That individual has been judged and his empire dismantled." Grainger simulated buffing his fingernails.

"What's this have to do with us?" Rivka asked.

"Forensics is our friend. We have all sides to deal with: the personal, their intent, and then the physical evidence to cement the case. It was amazing how much this thing told us after we asked the scientists who examined it what traces the creators might have left behind. Type of weld, including weld material, fingerprints because they built it in a place with an atmosphere and then transported it here. Air pockets trapped between welds showed us what the creators breathed. It gave us enough to find the planet, then the transport vessel, and finally, the entity who ordered it."

"Why would he go to such trouble?" Rivka wondered.

"One of the oldest rackets in the business. Protection. With the growth of Station 7, he wanted to establish a protection scheme; get paid to *not* rob them. He was trying to show them what he was capable of."

"Terrorism is a capital crime." Jael smiled. She hated terrorists.

"Yes. The individual saw the errors of his ways before his life's spark was extinguished." Grainger pointed to a ship holding position not far away. A Federation frigate.

"How do you rate the bigger ship?" Rivka asked.

Grainger pushed off the station before the jets came to life. "Rich parents left me money."

"Wait a minute!" Bustamove interrupted. "I never heard about a bomb outside the station."

"Of course not," Grainger replied. "It also reinforces what we do. Sometimes it's best to be high-profile, and then there are times where it is better to fly under the radar. When we board my ship, we'll review a case that needs to be handled delicately."

The Magistrates followed Grainger across the short open space. Red and Lindy took positions outside the entire group instead of staying at Rivka's elbows. When their duties expanded, they had to expand, too. Red was less than comfortable knowing that someone had been able to attach a bomb to the outside of the station he called home.

"How was the bomb discovered?" Red asked.

"Maintenance bots. They scour the surface multiple times daily. They noticed the installation as it was happening, and Lexi jammed the activation signal while technicians disarmed the bomb and removed the explosives. It was a threat for a very small window of time. Have no fear that the right people were on top of it from the start. They involved me later because it was outside of any other legal jurisdiction and the military didn't want to heavy-hand it. Magistrates keep the peace. I think we'll see our role in this area expanding away from cool palace murders to interplanetary concerns."

"You're harshing my buzz," Buster replied. "I like a good cozy mystery."

"Who doesn't? I'll still work my mojo to get us those cases when they appear in the daily feed."

"Bullshit!" Rivka declared, quickly realizing that she'd spoken out loud. A couple helmets turned toward her, making the owners veer off-course. They struggled to straighten themselves out. "I'm okay with you getting us those cases, but declaring that you have mojo is beyond the pale."

Snickers and snorts greeted Rivka's hasty recovery.

CHAPTER TWO

"I'd say that was a good effort," Jael offered. A few crusts remained from the twenty pizzas. It hadn't been a formal challenge to finish them, but the group had acted as if it were. Competitive to the last, they forced it down and then reclined in the oversized lounge of Grainger's frigate. A crew of four ran the ship, but they remained on the bridge or in engineering, leaving the Magistrates to themselves.

"It must get lonely," Rivka remarked softly. Grainger forced his eyes open since he'd started to drift off.

"I don't know what you mean." His voice was sleepy, but he was focused intently on Rivka. She reached toward him, and he crossed his arms. "Don't be zombieing me."

She bit her tongue, but the answer was clear in his expression. Theirs *was* a lonely profession. No one welcomed the Magistrates. Finish the case, mete out Justice, if warranted, and move on. Like in the movies about the Old West that had been brought from Earth. *Tombstone* was one of her favorite videos and although she knew it was fiction, she embraced it as a real representation. The Marshals had been a select few, just like the Magistrates.

There was only the inner circle. Everyone else was on the outside, held at arm's length.

By giving her a bodyguard and a crew of friends, he had spared her. She expected it was intentional. The others had all been Rangers first, as far as she knew. They had been operating independently for most of their very long lives.

But not her. "Thank you," she mouthed to Grainger. He looked uncomfortable with the gratitude.

Red excused himself to go to the bathroom, but his nefarious reason was revealed with a ship-shaking belch. When he returned, everyone was looking at him. "You heard that?" he asked, looking sheepishly away. "When do we land? Or a better question is, can I get some rack time before we leave the ship?"

Rivka nodded her approval. Red had been paying attention while she tried to shape questions that would give her the answer she was looking for.

"You have plenty of time, Red. We can't Gate too close to the planet. We'll be in the Opheramin system momentarily, but it'll take a while to navigate their traffic control system. Sleep fast. We'll let you know when we're getting ready to go," Grainger answered.

Lindy left with Red to find their cabin.

"You have number twelve," Grainger called after them.

"You may want to turn on some background music," Rivka suggested.

"Why?"

"Their relationship is young, and they act like newlyweds."

"Ah. Yes. That. Beau, please play my rock opera playlist." Guitars screamed, a lilting soprano wove her voice into the complex melody, and drums hammered at a high rate of speed. "Reduce the volume by ninety percent!"

The music dissolved into the background.

"I think I shall be forever scarred, emotionally and physically, from having heard that," Jael declared.

"Better than the alternative. Trust me," Rivka suggested.

"Back to the mission—"

"Case," Rivka corrected.

"Back to the case," Grainger continued without missing a beat. "Opheramin is not a new addition to the Federation, but we have little interaction. Our case is one of cloning."

"As distasteful as that is," Rivka chimed in, "it's not illegal, unfortunately."

"Humans."

"Oh. That would be a violation of Federation Law, Title 11, Section 10, Sentient Experimentation. I believe the punishment is five years' incarceration, a steep fine, forfeit and destruction of all materials, and name struck from professional registers. The purveyors become broke nobodies five years behind current technology."

Buster tried to lean forward, but his stomach fought him. He patted it happily and leaned back instead. "Are we supposed to have shit like that memorized?"

Grainger snickered and shook his head. He tapped his temple. "That's why we have these devices, so our AIs and EIs can tell us. Are you up to date?"

Rivka smiled. "Upgraded to the latest military comm package. My whole team is. We have yet to practice with them, though, since someone whisked us away at the beginning of our two weeks of downtime." Rivka stabbed her finger at Grainger.

"Training is training, even though this is a real case. I don't have the answer, so we'll look at it together. Go through the thought process of how this is or is not a criminal violation, and who gets punished? There are four clones from a single human. They are identical. There may be five clones and no human, but two of them have been murdered. What do we do, and to whom?"

"DNA?" Chi suggested.

"Already done. Identical." Grainger crossed his arms again and looked at the Magistrates. They were lost in thought.

"I could do my thing on them," Rivka said softly.

"I'm okay with shortcuts, but this is training. No one would learn anything if you did that. I'll need you to wear gloves throughout."

"I can still sense emotions without touching, but they have to be strong, and they're usually unclear."

"If you get something, don't tell us. No cheating, so you'll be more on the outside looking in, Rivka."

The thought of a clone's mind was intriguing. Could she tell it was a clone? "I need to see if I can tell a clone from the real thing."

"After we've tried it the hard way."

"Entering Opheramin space. There is less traffic than usual, which means we'll be landing in under two hours," Beau reported.

"Prepare yourselves," Grainger said. "We hit the ground running."

Red and Lindy were first off the frigate. They carried rail-guns, wore their ballistic vests, and carried small back-packs with additional security equipment in the form of reloads and weapons.

Grainger was next out, feeling weird about following someone else out of his own ship. The others fell in behind, with Rivka bringing up the rear, and they proceeded to where a small bus was waiting. The efficiency of the AIs in coordinating air traffic control, ground services, trans-portation, and meetings was unrivaled. None of the Magis-trates could imagine doing it themselves.

The outer hatch closed after Rivka passed through, and she paused to watch the ship seal itself. She took in the azure sky, and the sun's morning warmth. Green trees lined the small spaceport, making it look more like a park than a monument to interstellar travel.

Maybe that was the intent. Welcome the travelers home and show them what they were missing. Rivka agreed; it felt like home.

She'd fallen behind, leaving Red and Lindy in the open, their eyes in constant motion as they searched for threats to their charge. Grainger waved to get her attention, and she hurried to join the others.

Red and Lindy were last on the bus. She sat up front and Red took the back.

Rivka sat behind Lindy. "Thanks for joining the team, Lindy," Rivka told her. The young woman turned in her seat to face the Magistrate.

"Thank you for having me. I was doubtful about the

Pod-doc, especially after it added twenty-freaking-kilos! But as long as the weight stays distributed like it's supposed to, I guess it'll be okay. Red likes it." She waved to the big man in the back, and his cheeks flushed. "I had to buy a whole new wardrobe, which blew all the money I had. I'm embarrassed to ask, but can I maybe get an advance?"

Rivka looked pointedly at Grainger. "We changed her body so much she has to buy new clothes, and then we make her pay for them? That's unconscionable."

Grainger's expression never changed.

"Wait a minute, did I forget to transfer your cut from Red's fight on S'Korr?" Rivka didn't wait for an answer, just pulled out her datapad and started tapping. "Dammit!"

"You bet on your bodyguard?" Jael wondered loudly enough for everyone to hear.

"No *shit* I bet on him. You want me to bet against him?"

"That's not what I meant. You served up your man in a fight to the death to make some extra money?"

"To the untrained eye it might appear that way, but it was really the Federation standing up for human decency. And Red won, pulling in an extra eighteen grand that we split evenly amongst the crew." Rivka ducked her head. "It was evenly split until I forgot to send out everyone's cut. To make myself feel better, I'm throwing my cut into the kitty. Six thousand credits each. And there you are." Rivka pointed at Grainger. "And the Federation should pay for her new wardrobe, or at least give her a clothing allowance. We tend to get blaster scorching, cuts, and blood on our stuff."

Rivka displayed her Magistrate's jacket to highlight the

blaster scoring that she carried like a badge of honor. Grainger stuck his finger through a hole in the chest of his jacket. "An old-time slug. Hurt like hell; went right through my heart."

"You never mentioned that part when you were trying to recruit me..."

Chi and Buster choked as they laughed, bent nearly double. Jael chuckled and shook her head.

"'Recruited.' What an interesting word choice! I think what you meant to say we saved you from Jhiordaan. Yes, that is what 'recruited' meant. Getting shot in the heart is less traumatic than the prison planet." Grainger didn't look happy.

"High Chancellor Wyatt has seen me in my underwear," Lindy interjected, instantly stopping the degenerating conversation. Jael fell into the aisle between the seats, joining Chi and Buster in not being able to speak. Red was wide-eyed in disbelief.

Grainger tried to maintain his scowl, but failed. He had to look away as Lindy smiled beatifically.

Rivka winked at her.

"Got your back, Magistrate," Lindy whispered.

When the vehicle arrived, Red hurried to the front, resting a gentle hand on his girlfriend's shoulder while he looked out the front window to assess their surroundings before disembarking. "The building's entrance is right in front of us. No dawdling. Follow Lindy straight into the building. I'll be to the right between you and the nearest location where shooters could hide."

Red was first off the bus and took his position, railgun at the ready. Lindy led the Magistrates toward the door.

Rivka stayed close behind, but the others drifted. A statue with a plaque drew Jael's attention. A small kiosk demanded Chi and Buster's attention. When Grainger, the last off the bus, saw the statue, he joined Jael in reading the dedication to the planet's first governor, Beilton Opher.

Red signaled for them to go, but no one was watching. Lindy went through the doors while Rivka looked over her shoulder, discovering that the others weren't following. She walked back into the open area.

Red, can you hear me? Rivka asked using her implanted comm chip.

Roger, he replied. She sensed that he was unhappy. *I know I'm supposed to protect the Magistrate no matter where she goes or what she does. It's not my position to tell you that you can't do something. That being said, can you get these people inside?*

I'll do what I can. Rivka smiled at her bodyguard's exasperation.

"Guys," Rivka called when she got to the kiosk. "I'm pretty sure there's nothing you need."

Chi looked up, his hand full of trinkets and candy. "Need? No. Want? Yes. Buying? Yes." He dropped his treasures on the small counter, and an automated system dragged them one by one into a bag. He waved his chip at the unit and a green light signaled that the transaction was complete. A mechanical arm handed him the bag.

Buster bought a physical magazine. "What are you getting that for, a museum display?"

"The bathroom," he replied with a smile.

Rivka stared open-mouthed. For a moment, she was one with Red's frustration. "In the building, please. You're killing my bodyguards slowly, like the old water torture—one drip of intransigence at a time."

"Ooh! A statue." Buster started walking that way, but Rivka grabbed his arm and steered him toward the door. Chi removed a piece of candy and took a tentative bite, then chewed happily.

Grainger and Jael strolled through the open area, not in a hurry, but at least they were headed toward the building where they'd meet with the local law enforcement and judicial team.

Rivka gave the guys a friendly shove. "Don't make me kick your asses in front of the entire planet. Imagine the embarrassment. Come on, you're going to give Red heart failure, and where would that leave me?"

"Six thousand credits richer?" Chi suggested, still chewing. His smile had disappeared as he fought with the gooeyness in his mouth that threatened to remove all his teeth.

"Serves you right." Rivka punched him in the arm and nodded to Red. He hustled to meet her at the door, holding it open while his eyes continued to scan the area. He walked through, letting the door close on the lollygagging Magistrates. Lindy was over to the side talking with three uniformed locals.

Grainger approached.

"Magistrate," an older female said, "we'll escort you upstairs. I'm sorry, but no one can be armed around the holding cells so your personal security will have to remain behind."

Rivka joined them. "Are you familiar with Federation Law, Appendix D, Chapter Seven, Section 1 as it relates to armed guards for heads of state? That law applies to Magistrates as well. Wherever we go, we will be armed for our defense. As a Federation signatory, Opheramin will comply with this law. It supersedes planetary or local law."

"But if no one is armed, we're all safer," the guard countered.

"If we're the only ones armed, we'll be safest," Grainger suggested.

"But if the detainees break out, they could take your weapons."

"If the detainees break out, then the very last day of their existence will be filled with much pain. Have you ever heard the saying that in the land of the blind, a one-eyed man is king?"

"I have not."

"We're not going to let this delay us. We'll be heading upstairs now. The tenth floor, I believe?"

"You can't go armed," the guard said, interposing his body between the Magistrates and the elevator.

Grainger held up one finger while he removed his datapad from his jacket. "Beau, connect me to the governor's office, please."

"I have the executive assistant on the line," the EI replied after a few moments.

"This is Magistrate Grainger. I'd like to speak with the governor, please."

"He's not available," came a cold reply. Grainger's nostrils flared.

Rivka stepped to the side and accessed her datapad. The security personnel started to fidget, and Red appeared at Lindy's side.

"By Federation Law, we are permitted armed access anywhere on Opheramin. We need the governor to let the people here know that. You understand what 'failure to comply' means?"

"The governor is not available," the voice reiterated. "Why is it so important to be armed?"

Grainger thought his head was going to explode.

"No one is armed on Opheramin. We are a peaceful society. We have very little violent crime."

"'Very little' is still more than zero, and Magistrates tend to bring out the worst in people," Grainger argued.

The elevator door opened and an old female appeared. She shuffled out, waving and smiling as if she were greeting old friends.

"Magistrates?" she asked, even though she knew the answer. Grainger nodded and closed the link to the governor's office. He wasn't going to get anywhere using that approach, but before he closed the pad, he told Beau to report the violation and levy the maximum fine against the government, pending a final review by the High Chancellor.

"I'm Rivka Anoa, and this is Grainger," Rivka said, reaching for the female's hand. The thoughts and emotions the Magistrate picked up were of the case, the nice weather, and how attractive Grainger was. Rivka couldn't help but smile. Grainger picked up on Rivka's positive impression.

"I'm Senior Jurist Pasifa. Titles! I'm sorry. Call me 'Pass,' please."

Grainger shook the female's hand. She held onto it for

far longer than she'd held Rivka's hand. Grainger didn't seem to notice.

"When I saw this case appear, I knew we had to come," Grainger started. "It is unique in many ways. It could set a new precedent regarding how we, the Federation, deal with..." he stopped himself before he started discussing case details in an open area.

"Come with me and let's get started." Pass turned toward the elevators, but the local guard stopped her.

"They are armed, and I'm sorry, Senior Jurist, but they can't enter the building with weapons."

"On my personal authority—" she started, but was stopped by a shake of the guard's head.

Grainger bit his lip. He wasn't worried about their security, and had already started the process of fining the government. He wondered why he was being so difficult about getting Red and Lindy approved to go with them.

"Will you guarantee our weapons will remain secure if we leave them with you?" Grainger asked. Red clenched his teeth, and Lindy narrowed her eyes.

"Yes, of course."

Grainger tipped his chin to Red., and Rivka nodded without saying anything. Red drew a full breath before removing his pack and stuffing his railgun in. He added other weapons from around his body. Lindy put her weapons in as well until the pack was overflowing. Red shoved it at the local guard, who struggled with the weight of it.

"Don't lose our stuff," Red growled.

"Now, you're the king," Grainger said in a low voice before motioning for the senior jurist to lead on.

CHAPTER THREE

Before the elevator reached the top floor, Rivka handed Red her neutron pulse weapon. "Take care of this for me, will you?"

He grinned. "Of course." He tucked the small flashlight-looking weapon into his pocket. In his other pocket, he had an oversized folding knife.

Lindy had one, too. They had no intention of giving up *all* their weapons and were pleased to see that Rivka hadn't submitted either.

One team. One fight. The bad guys were out there somewhere, watching for the opportunity to strike. Red could never be off his game.

Or unarmed.

And with Lindy, he had a second set of eyes. Two for the price of one. Keeping peace in the universe brought the attention of too many enemies of humanity. Red was happy that Rivka never hesitated to reduce the numbers of those who embraced evil.

Maybe they were just psychotic, but in the end, those

who confronted the Magistrates—any of them—ended up taking a dirt nap when all was said and done, because more was done than said.

The tenth floor was painted off-white and had no decorations, being both sparsely furnished and austere. The doors and bars broached no question as to the purpose of this part of the building. Someone's moans sounded down the corridor.

Five Magistrates, two bodyguards, and the senior jurist waited as someone behind a heavy glass screen punched a button to open the main door. Beyond, there was a set of bars which wouldn't open until the first door had closed. The small space wouldn't fit eight people.

Red shouldered past the Magistrates into the space, then Pass, Grainger, and Rivka squeezed in and shut the door. The bars slid to the side, and they proceeded to the other side. The process was repeated, and when the final four joined the first group, Pasifa led them down a corridor away from the cells. The first two doors were open, showing small interrogation chambers. Each contained a table with a single chair on each side.

Rivka frowned and turned to the group. Jael was frowning, too. Chi and Buster didn't look happy. Grainger folded his arms across his chest. Pass started to look uncomfortable.

"For a peaceful planet, it seems like Opheramin treats its suspects harshly," Grainger said what they were thinking.

Pass pursed her lips before replying, "Maybe it's because suspects and crime are so little of what we do. We find the idea distasteful, and the people in here aren't just suspects. They don't come here until we are nearly certain that they were the one who committed the transgression."

"'Nearly certain' isn't the same as 'convicted,' Senior Jurist," Grainger replied. "Can we see the three suspects, please?"

Pasifa nodded while looking down. "Wait here." She shuffled away.

"This is like an old-time nut house. If you weren't crazy when you got here, you will be soon," Chi suggested.

"What we have to do is determine if one of these three is the original human, or if all three are clones and the human was one of the two who died. Then we have to adjudicate the existence of the clones. What happens to them, assuming that none of the three were responsible for the death of the other two?"

"What a shit sandwich." Jael tossed her head as she contemplated the case. She removed her datapad and started tapping.

"This is training." Grainger scowled. "There is nothing that's cut and dried. We have to dig out the good from the bad and get to the truth. When Rivka joined our ranks, she showed us what real lawyering is all about. We need more of that, so here we are. She gets to help us work through this."

"When were you going to tell me that?" Rivka demanded.

"How about now?"

She closed her eyes and sighed, then removed her gloves from her pocket. "Let the show begin."

The sound of approaching footsteps drew their attention. Behind the senior jurist, three identical-looking men trundled along in shackles and chains with a single guard behind them. He didn't appear to have a weapon. Rivka glanced at Red. He had the neutron pulse weapon concealed in his hand while trying to look casual. Lindy was tense. When the three arrived, she instructed one of them to remain in the hallway, while the other two went to separate interrogation rooms.

"You can interview them one at a time," Pass offered.

Grainger pointed at Rivka, Red, and Chi and then to the second door. "You take that one." They headed in and closed it behind them. "With me." The rest entered the second interrogation room. The senior jurist remained in the hallway with the lone guard and the remaining suspect.

Rivka leaned against the wall, Red looming large next to her. They looked at the table where Chi faced an exact copy of the two other suspects.

He set his datapad on the table and activated it. "What's your name?"

"My name is Gregar Deiston," the suspect replied evenly.

"Do you know why you're here?"

"You think I killed my brother."

"I don't think anything of the sort. Two people who look exactly like you have been murdered. We want to make sure you aren't the next target." Chi rolled the words smoothly off his tongue. "You have to admit that you are safe within this building."

"Then why the shackles?" the man asked.

"So the other prisoners don't think this has become a luxury hotel." Chi smiled at the man. Rivka fought back a snort.

"You think I did it?"

"I think that *you* think you're a criminal. It's my job to determine how many crimes you've committed. Let's start with cloning. The very existence of a human clone means that a crime has been committed. That's one strike."

"Since when is existing a crime? I had no control over any of it. I was simply born. Being born is a crime in the vaunted Federation?"

"You admit that you are a clone, then. That helps. Why did you kill your creator?"

"I'm sorry, you're not very good at this. Are you new? Is this your first day?" the suspect snarked, leaning back and rolling his eyes.

"I was seeing if you were paying attention. Describe the events that happened ten days ago in the time leading up to the discovery of the two bodies that looked just like you."

"No," the man replied before yawning. "I'm tired. Please return me to my luxury suite."

Chi lunged forward and pounded a fist on the table. Gregar flinched and then smiled.

"Tell me what happened," Chi ordered.

Rivka was beginning to think the suspect was right. Chi *wasn't* very good at this. He didn't appear to have reviewed the file to check known facts first in order to gauge the suspect's reactions, to better identify when he was lying.

Everyone lies, Rivka remembered Jay's words. *Of course, they do. If they're guilty, they have every incentive to lie, and even if they're innocent, not all truth is good truth.*

27

Chi was still leaning across the table when she tapped him on the shoulder. He straightened up, looking surprised.

"I'd like to take a seat, please." Rivka pointed with her eyes at the chair. Chi stepped to the side and she sat down. "Let's see where we were."

She handed Chi's datapad to him and put hers in its place.

"If you would be so kind, could you confirm a few details for me?" She fumbled with her screen for a few moments before declaring victory. "Aha! You live at 342 Bearplatz?"

Rivka looked up when Gregar failed to answer.

"342 Bearplatz?" she asked again. He only looked at her. "I'll take that as a yes. You drive a...let me see. I thought I saw a vehicle registration here somewhere..." More fumbling with her datapad. She dropped it on the table, apologized, and picked it up again.

"I don't have a car. None of us do."

"Are you sure?" Rivka asked in surprise. "I'm sure I saw a registration here somewhere."

"None of us do. You're barking up the wrong tree."

"I thought I saw one. I must have been mistaken." Rivka leaned back before digging into her pad again. "For the five of you, only one identification card was issued. Which one of you has that?"

"I'm sorry?"

"Which one of you carries the card?"

"We all do," he answered. "And none of us do."

"Please clarify. I'm just a barrister, and not that smart. You might have to spell things out a little more simply."

He squinted at her.

"Did you forget your glasses in your luxury suite? Maybe we can send the bellhop for them," Rivka suggested.

"I don't wear glasses. None of us do."

"You don't need to answer for the others. None of my questions are about them. They are all about you. Do you carry an ID card?"

He held up empty hands, his chains rattling against the table.

"Is that a no?"

The suspect nodded. "Yes, it's a no."

"Douchebag," Chi mumbled.

"I don't like him," Gregar stated as he glared at Cheese Blintz.

"I don't care who you do or don't like. That's none of my business. I *do* care that you are being evasive. As a Magistrate, I take that as a sign that you are a criminal, and are poorly hiding that fact." She stood to look down her nose at him. "That's all the questions we have for now."

She left the room without looking back, expecting Red and Chi to follow her. Red was close on her heels, but Chi shut the door, remaining with the suspect.

It wasn't long before Grainger and the others came out of their room. "Want to give this one a try?" the Magistrate asked before noticing the absence. "Where's Chi?"

Rivka pointed with her chin.

Grainger pushed past and yanked the door open. Inside, a werewolf loomed over the table snapping at the suspect's face. Gregar was against the wall and had nowhere to go. His jaws were clenched, and his chained hands held up as if they alone could fend off the beast.

"Holy shit!" Rivka exclaimed. Red's eyes shot wide and he raised the neutron pulse weapon. Rivka put a hand on his arm.

"Stop that and get out here!" Grainger ordered, and closed the door before Pass could see.

Grainger was not amused, but he shook off the scene and smiled. "Let me guess. That guy said his name was Gregar something or other, and referred to his brothers. You think he's a clone, but you're not sure."

"I think this one's a clone because he slipped and said that he didn't have ID. Only one of them does, and that's the sample donor. Would the real Gregar Deiston please stand up?" Rivka offered. "Now, let's talk about what the fuck I just saw."

Grainger held a finger to his lips. Pasifa wasn't far away.

"Soon," he replied with a wink. She wanted to choke the soon out of him.

Chi, too. Words were going to be had, and it wasn't going to be pleasant.

CHAPTER FOUR

"Can you secure these two? Make sure they can't talk to each other or the third 'brother,' as they call themselves? We'll get to the last one shortly, but we need to share our notes and impressions from the first two conversations," Grainger told Pass.

"What was going on in the interrogation room? If you were torturing the suspect, I will have you hauled out of here!" Pasifa declared.

"We don't believe in torture any more than you do. We believe in intimidation, mind you, but not torture. The information is too sketchy when people speak while in pain. Under threat, they have a tendency to lie more poorly, from what we've found." Grainger smiled. He knew she had no power to expel the Magistrates, but she could make it hard for them to do their jobs.

In this instance it was only training, but there was a real case that needed to be resolved. Grainger considered his interaction with the senior jurist as a training opportunity every bit as important as interrogating the intransigent suspects. Even as old as he was, there was always more to learn.

He was also learning about herding cats. Grainger had never had all the Magistrates on one mission before. He had expected that their strengths would complement each other and show the power of the team approach as an option for exceptionally difficult cases. He was still kicking himself for sending Rivka alone on her RICO case. Twenty planets with a wealthy godfather, one with his own fleet of warships as the prize at the end. Grainger would never admit the mistake, but Rivka's performance had shown him that her approach might trump what the Magistrates had been doing before.

Lawyering first. And that was why he had brought them on this case. Training to be better lawyers.

"You're the best of us," he said, looking at Rivka and mistakenly speaking out loud.

She looked at him from under raised brows.

The door opened and a disheveled Chi appeared. "Sorry. What did I miss?"

"We were about to ask you that same question," Grainger said, turning away from the penetrating gaze of Rivka's golden-blue hazel eyes.

"Giving something different a shot," Chi replied sheepishly. "I didn't get anything else."

He smiled reluctantly, only to find Rivka glaring at him.

"Sorry," he mumbled.

"I can't believe none of you sandy little buttholes told me about that. Who else? Come on." Rivka reached toward Grainger.

"Oh, no you don't, Zombie!" He backpedaled, bouncing off the wall and running into Lindy.

"Take your medicine," the bodyguard told him.

"Cats and dogs. No wonder my damn skin is crawling," Red muttered.

Pass couldn't follow what they were saying. She shook her head and snapped her fingers. Two guards appeared to remove the suspects and take them to separate detention cells. The third was placed in a holding area not far away.

Gregar jangled his chains as he walked past Chi. "Am I the one going crazy or are you?" he asked, before the guard nudged him to keep walking. The Magistrate didn't answer.

"We could use a debriefing room if you have one available," Grainger suggested hopefully. Pass pointed to the interrogation rooms and walked away, still shaking her head as if the Magistrates were speaking in tongues.

Red held the door to the small room with the single table and two plain chairs open. "We'll wait out here. That should give you enough space."

The Magistrates entered, and Red dutifully closed the door behind them. He stepped to the side so he couldn't hear what they were saying, unless they started to shout—which he expected.

Collum Gate

The delegation from Y'eaton had decided to go upscale to celebrate their negotiations with the Yollins. They'd found that trying to deal with Yollins on Yoll was problematic and fruitless. The only way to negotiate a border issue was through an embassy on an alien planet. Collum Gate served that purpose nicely.

The Y'eaton had four legs, a shell, and antennae sticking out of their heads. They also seemed more comfortable in the presence of the upper-class Yollins, who also had four legs. Their mandibles were unique and intimidating, but not as intimidating as the Shrillexians. Their spikes projected from their bodies somewhat like those of a porcupine, but were hard and metal-like.

The delegation discovered two other groups eating at the establishment, which served a variety of dishes to tantalize almost any palate.

"Well done, Zaria. Your skill at discovering what the Yollins wanted has helped us move this treaty farther forward today than in the past year. In one day! I can't even express how pleased I am with the progress," an older Y'eaton said.

"It makes my heart soar with joy to hear your appreciation, Mister Ambassador. Everything we do is for a better Y'eaton."

The ambassador smiled pleasantly at the syrupy words, secretly wishing that the meals would arrive so they could get down to meaningless small talk.

"Ah! It looks like our lunch has passed the chef's watchful eye and is on its way." A server approached slowly, balancing the tray with five separate platters loaded with a variety of fare. The shock wave hit the server from behind. Riding the front of the wave was a curtain of metal shards that turned him into a spray that splattered across the delegation.

A spray laced with razor-sharp metal. The delegation

from Y'eaton was turned into mash, their shells providing no protection. They were thrown through the front entrance of the restaurant, and into the street beyond.

The tables on either side were untouched, as if a giant shotgun had been fired from within the kitchen. A hole in the counter suggested the device had been secreted behind it, as if someone had known the delegation would sit at that table.

In a restaurant that catered to alien diplomats, the chance that someone important who wasn't from Collum Gate would sit at that particular table approached one hundred percent.

Who were the targets—the delegation from Y'eaton or just any aliens?

Rivka crossed her arms and leaned against the wall. Grainger offered her a seat, but she shook her head. Jael stood next to her as if they were getting ready to play a game of boys against the girls. Grainger pulled out a chair and spun it around to sit with his forearms resting on the back.

"Would all the werewolves in here raise your hands, please?" Grainger was the first to put his in the air, and the others followed one by one.

"You have got to be shitting me. What a triple-decker ass-blast!" Rivka exclaimed, stabbing a finger at Grainger to blame him for not telling her sooner.

"We were all products of a time long past. We had the gene. We were injured and saved by the blood of a werewolf, a Ranger, who dug our sorry asses out of an ambush gone bad. And then we were further healed and upgraded by the Pod-doc," Grainger explained. "We joined them in their missions to mete out Justice, going out on our own. But since they disbanded shortly afterward, we didn't quite get the full training. In our previous lives, the werewolf came in handy, but as Magistrates there's no need, unless you're Cheese Blintz and believe that the beast within will convince perps to come clean."

"*All* of you?" Rivka tried not to sound hurt.

"Does it change who we are or what we do?" Grainger held a finger up to stop Rivka from replying. "Does it change anything besides your perception of us, that you didn't know a secret from our pasts?"

"You could have told me."

"When was the first time you killed someone?" Grainger asked.

"What?" Rivka fired back.

"The first time, and don't lie to us."

"It's what brought me to you."

"Now you're lying to yourself." Grainger shook his head. Rivka didn't understand. "When you were a child. Remember the blood?"

Rivka sagged like a deflating balloon. She covered her face with her hands as if trying to block the memories from intruding, but she couldn't stop them.

"It was the same thing," she said, her voice suddenly shaking. Her hands remained in front of her, making it sound like she was mumbling. "Like the perp who was set free at trial. I blacked out, coming to with a bloody knife in my hands. I was six years old. A man had tried to take me away. The police found me and brought me home. No one said a word. We had bean-burgers that night, with chips. I remember it as if it were yesterday. I could feel that my parents were upset, but they put on brave faces. That was before they were lost. How did you know?"

"Bethany Anne shared it with the High Chancellor, and he shared it with me when the time was right. For a moment it made me pity you, but we don't thrive that way. I met the adult Rivka, and that's all I need to know. I said you were the best of us because you have taken the law and made it foundational to our work. We have been using the law to keep the peace, but in a case like this one—clones? I don't know what to do because I don't care. I don't see how it hurts the Federation, but you do. You know the ramifications and probably have an idea what to do about it, fully supported by precedent to help shape a future that makes sense."

Rivka continued to look at the floor.

Jael raised her hand. Grainger nodded.

"For the record, I haven't changed into a werewolf in over a decade."

Buster started speaking. "My answer would be to put them away and be done with it. Remove the perp's chance to use his knowledge for evil. If we put away two clones, so be it. I know that the law would rather guilty men be free than innocent ones be punished. I don't see where we can take that risk. If an innocent gets caught in the dragnet, he's sacrificing for the greater good. That makes sense to me. The military sacrifices. Police make sacrifices. Even people who work in the service industry makes sacrifices."

Rivka crossed her arms, not defensively, but in relaxation as the conversation became something she could sink her mental teeth into.

"I'm with Buster. There are crimes here. I'd ask Philko to give me the language, and I'd shoehorn it in. Don't you think they are guilty of something?" Chi wondered.

"We can't just blast them into nonexistence for being assholes," Jael said. Grainger looked at her sideways. "Hey! A girl can change her mind."

"I'd put them on ice for a month or a year and then come back and see what they had to say," Grainger suggested.

"What does the DNA show?" Rivka asked.

"That the five are identical," Grainger replied.

"Can we transmit the DNA data to Ankh? He and Erasmus will be able to dig deeper into it, and it won't be one hundred percent identical. There's a margin of error in every DNA sample. The five will be different in unique ways, but all within the standard for identification. I'm sure the five will come up as the same person, but they will be slightly different."

Grainger accessed his datapad. "Beau is sending it now." He put the datapad away. "What else?"

"We need to look at the bodies. What will the autopsy tell us? Were they murdered? If so, were they killed by the same person? We have multiple issues. Let's break them down, looking at the most heinous first. We have at least two human clones, right here, right now, and they are creepy as hell. Gregar—the one we talked with, anyway— was right. Existence is not a crime. Being a drug addict is not a crime, but buying illegal drugs is. Being a clone is not a crime. A clone had no choice in the matter. He exists. Do we incarcerate them, or do we give them separate identities, like we would have for identical twins? But at least identical twins have different fingerprints and iris scans. Is that stuff identical for the members of Team Gregar?"

Grainger brought out his datapad.

"I'll save you the time. They are," Rivka said. "The locals didn't do brain scans. After their creation, their minds would have started unique development. Even something as simple as looking at an event from different sides of the same room would create unique memories and change how the being thinks. That is my premise, but will it lead us to the real Gregar, if he is still alive?"

"I'll order scans for each of the three," Grainger said.

"Maybe we can question them during the scan and see what their response is to questions about the murder."

"We can't put a clone away for being a clone, but we can lock up a murderer." Rivka watched the others nod.

"*That's* what I'm talking about!" Grainger declared, raising his hands to get high-fived by the others.

"You weren't talking about that at all," Rivka stammered.

Grainger stood. "Who wants lunch?" he asked, opening the door.

"I'm starving!" Chi replied instantly.

"Nice work, Zombie. Chow sounds good. Count me in," Jael added.

"You da bomb, Zombie." Buster nodded once and walked out. Red looked into the room to find Rivka still leaning against the wall.

"Are you okay?"

"They have the attention spans of twelve-year-olds!"

"At least you're not running," Red suggested with a shrug. "Did I hear something about lunch? I'm pretty hungry, and I bet you are, too."

"I know *I* am," Lindy called from the hallway.

"I shall submit to the group's physical needs, even though we have work to do."

"Who are you kidding?" Grainger asked from somewhere out of sight. "You hate working on an empty stomach more than we do."

"*Fine!*" she stated, almost shouting.

"You're in for it now," Jael told Grainger.

CHAPTER FIVE

They couldn't get the scans until the next day, so Grainger thanked the senior jurist, telling her that they would retire for continued collaboration until the equipment was set up.

Red and Lindy recovered their gear, skeptical at first, but when everything was accounted for, the big man thanked the security personnel for their diligence and their efforts to keep the Magistrates safe from harm.

Rivka kept a straight face throughout because she knew he didn't mean any of it.

"Your diplomatic skills are improving," she told him once they were back on board Grainger's frigate.

"I was hoping no one would notice. I hate that fawning crap. You want safe? Give me my fucking railgun!" he bellowed.

"Three weeks ago you had no railgun, and now it's your baby. Does it have a name?" Rivka pressed.

Lindy tried to stop her, but it was too late.

He smiled. "I call her 'Blazer.'" Lindy rolled her eyes. "What? You have a name for yours, too."

"Mabel," Lindy said softly.

"Mabel. And Blazer." Rivka looked from one body-guard to the other. "And my neutron pulse weapon?" She crooked a finger, and Red handed the weapon to her.

"'Delimiter,' or 'Dealy' for short."

"Not 'Death on a Stick?' Or maybe 'the Fucku-penheimer?'"

Red and Lindy shook their heads.

"Dealy. I feel like I should be offended, but that's for the weak of heart. What do you call your junk? No! Why the hell did I ask that? I still can't get the image of your junk on my shoulder out of my mind. I have to take a shower." Rivka hurried away.

"Your junk was on the Magistrate's shoulder?" Lindy asked.

"Yes. I was dying of heat stroke, and she carried me back to the ship. I've told you about this. It was fucking hot. Not just a little bit. Not uncomfortable-hot, but kill-you-hot."

"You've told me, but I like how you get so defensive every time you talk about it. It's sexy when men have a weakness."

"And women have to save me from it?"

"It's what we've been doing since the beginning of time, my invincible star warrior." She wrapped her arms around his neck, encouraging him to smile.

"I was raised to believe that men were the providers and could never show vulnerabilities. We have to be the pillar of strength, the bedrock on which the family is built," he tried to explain.

"But if you know that isn't true, why do you persist?"

"It's not an easy habit to break," he admitted. "I'm trying. Give me that much, and as long as you and Rivka keep reminding me, we'll get to where it will be second nature. And then if we ever have kids, we'll raise them differently. Mom and Dad, out there side by side blasting the ever-living shit out of bad guys."

Lindy chuckled. "Nice image." She met Red's eyes and looked deeply into them. "Weren't you the one who said the men had the women outnumbered on *Peacekeeper*? You, Chaz, Hamlet, Ankh, and Erasmus. Something like that. Five to three. 'We are manly men!'"

Red liked the way Lindy's eyes sparkled when she was giving him a hard time. She was making a valid point, though. He *had* said those very words. "Hamlet is the manliest of us all. That cat doesn't give a shit."

"And what's this bit about kids? I'm not even sure I'll let you be my boyfriend."

He brushed the hair from beside her eye and tucked it behind her ear. With the tip of his finger, he slowly and lightly traced the outside of Lindy's ear.

The next day, the team retraced their steps. Red wanted to vary the routine, but it hadn't become predictable yet. If there were a third day, he would insist they change the time, the bus, and the approach to the building.

Red and Lindy handed over their weapons without

being asked, even though it wasn't easy. The senior jurist wasn't waiting for them. They didn't need an escort, so they headed up.

They took the elevator in two groups. No one spoke as they contemplated what the day would bring. Red and Rivka were the first ones out, nearly running into Pasifa, who was rushing toward the elevator.

"I'm so sorry," she apologized. "I was helping the medical team get set up and lost track of time."

"Of course you were helping them," Rivka said with relief. "I thought we'd worn out our welcome, and that was the last thing we wanted. I brought you this—a pastry from my home planet. I hope the fabrication device on the ship has done it justice." Rivka offered the small bag with the treat inside.

Pass smiled and accepted the gift, graciously taking a small bite while her guests watched. She grinned and took a bigger bite. When she finished chewing, she lost her smile. "This is a nasty business. We don't want to be known as the clone planet."

"Has anything like this happened before?"

"Not to my knowledge," she replied. Rivka touched her arm and smiled warmly. Images of another case flashed through her mind.

Damn, there was! The images of a scientist being led away in shackles under the dark of night flashed through the senior jurist's mind.

Rivka would ask Beau to look into it as soon as she was free to send the request.

The senior jurist led the way through the halls, past cells where prisoners reclined, watching every move the visitors made. Rivka thought it odd that the space selected for the brain scans was beyond the detention area. Red carried Dealy, the neutron pulse weapon, in his hand. Lindy had her hand in a pocket where a knife was secreted. Rivka wondered how good the young woman was with it.

Grainger and Buster walked with their heads up, eyes darting around. Jael and Chi were also on edge.

"Excuse me." Rivka tapped Pasifa on the shoulder. "This is an interesting arrangement, with the cell block in the middle of the building. I've always seen them at the ends of corridors with only one way in or out."

"There *is* only one way out, and that's back the way we came. Unfortunately, this building wasn't originally meant for this purpose. As I said, we're a peaceful people. Crime is such an ugly mark."

Once through the cell block, the area opened up with larger rooms, one of which had a reclining medical chair with a heavy device that could be arranged around one's head. A team of two people in white scrubs was waiting. The computer interface was live.

After the introductions, one of the technicians said they were ready.

"Can you link this directly to our ship? Does it have an external capability?" Grainger asked, already tapping on his datapad.

"Of course," the technician replied. Grainger turned Beau loose, and within moments the uplink was established.

"Thank you. We'll parse the data separately. We'll need a baseline reading for an average person from Opheramin, if you could send that sometime as well."

"Yes, no problem." The technician was accommodating. While they waited for the first suspect, he accessed a baseline reading and transmitted it.

They didn't wait long before one of the Gregars arrived. They put him in the chair despite his protests.

"I refuse to give my permission for this invasive procedure. You are torturing me!" he screamed.

"We have different definitions of invasive, I think," Grainger mumbled. He leaned close to the shrieking man. "If you want to be throat-punched, keep screaming."

The threat had no effect.

"I don't want to do this, but to build trust, one simply must do as one says he will." In a flash, Grainger knife-handed the man in the throat. The noise instantly ceased. The suspect's hands were strapped to the arms of the chair, so he couldn't rub his injured neck. He started bobbing his head back and forth. "I told you to shut it, and now you need to hold your head still. I'm told they can get a reading even if you're unconscious, so even if you make me hit you again, we'll still get what we need. Maybe it will be easier that way."

Grainger made a fist and reared back. Gregar clenched his mouth shut and sat still. A technician tightened the piece around his head, and the scanning began. It took a total of five minutes from start to finish.

After the scan, Gregar glowered at the Magistrates. Grainger ordered, "Get him out of here, and bring in the next suspect, please."

The next version of Gregar arrived, readily took the seat, sat back, and relaxed. He was in the room for a total of seven minutes and didn't say a word the entire time. The Magistrates remained silent for the process as well.

"Next," Grainger declared when the second scan was finished.

The third Gregar Deiston was identical to the other two, but he wasn't. The look in his eyes was different. Rivka noticed and immediately moved forward, reaching out to touch him. Grainger stopped her. Jael, Chi, and Buster hovered as if each wanted some personal time with the suspect.

"I never had the pleasure of chatting with you as my brothers did. I feel left out," Gregar stated.

"We should paint numbers on their heads," Jael suggested.

"I suspect you are trying to determine if there are clones among us."

"We're trying to find the murderer of your so-called brothers," Rivka replied, standing casually to give the man the least number of physical cues.

"Then why are you talking to me?" he countered.

"You're the one doing the talking, but let's hook you up and get the test out of the way first," Grainger interrupted, nodding to the technician. Gregar shrugged and didn't fight the procedure.

Five minutes, and the final test was done. Grainger accessed his datapad and verified that Beau had the information. The EI immediately returned with a note that he'd received the analysis from Ankh and Erasmus.

Grainger pointed at Rivka and pantomimed typing on the datapad. She removed hers and accessed the information Ankh had sent. She skimmed it, since it was more than thirty pages, and tapped out a quick note.

In the middle of an interrogation. Please give me an executive summary.

She put her datapad away and looked up to find Gregar's gaze boring a hole in her. She smiled at him. "You're the one who got the identification card."

"We all carry the same card. The local government is less than accommodating to those who aren't able to present a birth certificate. We should all have our own so we don't run afoul of the law, which is our current plight. We've been held for far longer than the law allows. I insist that you let us go—me and my brothers."

Grainger smiled at Rivka. A gentle hand pushed her from behind. She laced her fingers behind her back and started to stroll around the suspect.

"Are you sure you understand the jurisdiction handling this case?" Rivka asked.

"Opheramin," Gregar replied with less confidence than his previous statement.

Rivka shook her head. "Federation law applies, specifically Title 11, Section 10 regarding sentient experimentation. All suspects can be held during the active investigation period. Is there any doubt that we, the Federation Magistrates, are actively investigating this case?" Rivka waited, but Gregar didn't answer.

Rivka continued her lecture. "No need to say anything, because I am right. You can consider this to be part of your legal education before you engage a lawyer. You'll be held for as long as we need to adjudicate this case, which we will do before we leave. Do you have any questions?"

"I guess you're going to do what you're going to do—use the law to bludgeon the little guy."

Rivka pursed her lips. Wrinkles appeared on her forehead as she assumed her contemplative face. "We use the law to protect people. You have not been bludgeoned, but should you be found guilty and the law calls for it, you will feel its full weight. The law is a framework in which civilized societies function. Don't ever forget that. One of you violated the law, and then one or more of you murdered your brothers. We will find who did it. There are other points of law, but I don't wish to bore you with technical details. Understand that you and your brothers, as you call them, are in a very dark place. The more we shine the light on you, the more we see."

She waved at the guard in the hallway to take this version of Gregar away.

"We'll be in touch." She smiled as he walked away, his expression no longer neutral.

Once he was gone, Jael started slow-clapping. "You used the law to bludgeon him without actually threatening him. Bravo, sister!"

"You bludgeoned that smug look right off his face," Buster remarked. They took turns clapping her on the back.

Grainger thanked the technicians as the group departed. The senior jurist remained silent, having watched the proceedings to make sure that Opheramin law was upheld. The Magistrates had made it clear that she was no longer in control. She realized that once she had called for help, she had passed the buck.

Maybe it had been her naiveté, having never referred a

case to the Federation for adjudication. Deep down inside, she didn't want this case. It was troubling, and after all, Opheramin was a peaceful planet...

"Imagine what you could have accomplished if you'd interrogated him while in the form of a werewolf!" Chi whispered.

"You can talk while you're changed?"

"Well, no," Chi stammered.

Rivka didn't bother to reply. She wanted to get back on board the frigate and dig into the report Ankh had sent, as well as look into the analysis of the brain scans. On the bus, she never once looked up from her datapad. The others looked out the window, taking in their surroundings. Red and Lindy watched for threats, cradling their railguns to bring them comfort and peace of mind.

Red and Lindy bracketed their Magistrate since she was studying and oblivious to everything around her. The other Magistrates left her alone.

"What's your ship's name?" Buster asked.

"Does it need a name?" Grainger replied with a shrug.

"Of course it needs a name!" Jael remarked. "I call mine *Starseeker's Chariot*."

"Your boat used to be a druggie's personal yacht. It'll hold one person comfortably, and you see it as a chariot?" Chi couldn't figure out how the name fit.

"Yes. That is the correct name. What do you call yours?"

"*Doomsayer's Deathride*," Chi shot back.

"Bullshit." Jael looked down her nose at him.

"Okay. It's called *Red Corvette*. Don't judge me."

"That is *all* I'm going to do."

"No. I don't have a name, and I don't think I need one. The frigate is hull number sixty-nine." Grainger tried not to smirk as he hurried into the ship. Jael rolled her eyes, and Chi and Buster groaned.

Rivka remained oblivious.

Once in the ship, Red put Rivka at a table with a comfortable chair before conducting a quick search of the ship. Lindy stood guard until the outer hatch closed and she received the thumbs-up.

The other Magistrates gathered around Rivka.

"Oh, jeez," she grumped. "Ankh wants to talk us through the data."

"What's wrong with that?"

Rivka chuckled. "Coffee for everyone!" she declared and headed for the galley. No one offered to help, and she didn't need it. She brought five mugs back.

"Can't you just order him to send the data?"

"No," Rivka answered. "My crew are all volunteers. We work as a team. No one is giving anyone orders."

Red snorted.

"I heard that!" Rivka pointed at him. He attempted his best innocent face. "And no one gives Ankh shit. He's one of the best in the universe at what he does. He may be a big-headed but tiny alien, but he's on my team. I will beat the living shit out anyone who gives him grief."

Grainger looked at her from beneath a single raised eyebrow.

"If I can't do it, I'll have Red and Lindy do it. Your ass will be beaten, so don't cross that line." Rivka looked from face to face, unconvinced that they were going to play nice. "Fuckers," she added for emphasis.

Nods suggested they would try.

Rivka handed out the coffee and brought up the main screen. Ankh's face appeared. It was live, but it could easily have been a single image. Ankh's expression was blank, and he didn't move.

"Thanks for the analysis, Ankh. Can you give us the executive summary up front and then maybe we can ask questions to fill in the blanks?" Rivka asked hopefully.

"No," he replied simply. "Let me start with the Single Nucleotide Polymorphisms. There are approximately ten million in the human genome. Ninety percent of these will be identical from one human to another. Needless to say," Ankh started.

But you're going to say it anyway, Rivka thought, joining her fellow Magistrates in taking a long sip of coffee.

"In the clones, there is well beyond a ninety-nine percent match. In fact, each of the DNA samples, including those from the two bodies in the morgue, were exactly the same, except in the minute area where they were different. There, each of the five was different. No single marker identified one of the five as more human than the others. All five are distinctly human.

"So I continued with the short tandem repeats, which were, expectedly, inconclusive. Since the SNP data was complete, I looked at the mitochondrial DNA to build an exact sequence. Despite their similarities, I expected to see differences deep within the strands."

Ankh stopped, and Rivka froze mid-sip. "Did we lose the connection?"

"No," Ankh replied.

"So what's your conclusion?" Rivka wondered.

"There are five clones."

"None of them is human?" Grainger blurted.

"All of them are human," Ankh replied.

"Is *one* more human than the others?" Rivka prodded.

"No."

"You've been a great deal of help, Ankh. Thank you! So, from what I hear you saying, we haven't found the human from which these five were cloned." Rivka crossed her arms as she started to descend into thought.

"I assume the original donor is dead."

The Magistrates focused on Ankh's face.

"What makes you say that?" Grainger asked.

"Because the cloning process in this instance, which included background data from the case file, suggests that it is a destructive technique using significant quantities of source material from the donor's organs. Namely, brain matter and internal organs."

"So you didn't need to do the analysis of their DNA at all?" Grainger's expression soured as he asked the question. Rivka bit her lip to keep from laughing.

"Human genome analysis is fascinating. I've been able to compare the samples to other human data that R2D2, the research and development unit, maintains. Fascinating."

Rivka purposefully took a slow sip of coffee, hiding her face behind her mug.

"Thank you, Ankh. You have been spectacular, and your information most enlightening. We have to go and lay down the law. I'll be home soon." Rivka quickly tapped her pad to turn off the screen and cut the signal.

"He couldn't have started with that?" Grainger asked.

"I told you," Rivka said. "But does it matter as much as the data he shared? I have it all here. I also have a quick brief on dealing with clones."

"Of course you do," Chi said. "That changes things."

"Not really," Rivka said, which stopped the others in their tracks. "We still have a murderer to find. We were always going to have to adjudicate the future of the clones, but now we don't get to chuck the original human into the hoosegow. Shame. That being said, who ran the cloning process if it wasn't the original guy? Maybe we have someone new to look for."

CHAPTER SIX

Immediately following Ankh's revelation, they made a trip to the morgue and then to the scene of the crime. "Why didn't we do this first?" Chi asked.

"Because this stuff will keep. Perps will keep changing their story, the more time you give them," Rivka replied. She'd been the one who insisted on interrogating the suspects first. Grainger had agreed with her logic.

When they reached the morgue and looked at the bodies, they got no additional insight. Rivka spent a total of five seconds examining the dead. She focused her attention on the one who conducted the autopsy, which on Opheramin, wasn't a doctor but a scientist. Still called a coroner, he talked about the details of the wound and made a guess as to how it could have been made.

"Blunt object from behind," Grainger surmised. "Same for both."

The scientist deflated with the simplification. "Pretty much."

"Same method for both suggests a single perp, but what

if the perps were identical clones?" Rivka pondered. "What about motive and opportunity?"

Rivka looked from one face to the next, but no one could answer. They'd read the investigative reports, but nothing had stood out. For Rivka, it wasn't what stood out, but the overall picture. It wasn't a single smoking gun, but an entire story. Too often there was a single clue that tied the suspect to the crime.

And then there were cases like this where none of it made sense. They were all guilty of something, but maybe none of them were.

"Why?" Rivka asked.

"There can be only one?" Grainger quoted from one of his favorite movies.

"Maybe it is as simple as that," Buster replied, fully engaged. Chi nodded, looking like he wanted to say something.

"Cheese Blintz? Come on, man, out with it," Grainger encouraged.

"The three in custody have gone to great lengths through their evasion to conceal the truth. To me, that suggests they are guilty. We can't catch them in a lie since they've said nothing, which was wise on their part. They don't need to incriminate themselves. As you so astutely pointed out before we started, we need to convict the guilty using evidence."

"And we still don't have any of that," Buster said. "I read the file. The fact that all five of them have identical fingerprints jumped out at me. How is that possible?"

"Beau?" Grainger asked his datapad.

"I would have said that it is not possible, but I will revise my opinion based on current evidence."

"That wasn't much help," Jael remarked. "Shall we explore the crime scene?"

"Beau, can you have the legal authorities meet us there to give us access, please?"

"I am contacting them now." The group waited for a full minute before Beau returned. "They will be there when you arrive."

"I don't know how you do it, but I like it. You are the epitome of efficiency, Mister Beau."

"Thank you. I—" Grainger cut him off and stuffed the datapad into his coat.

"Shall we?" He motioned for the others to lead the way. As usual, Red was the first one out the door.

The two-story set of rooms was within an apartment complex. It looked more like a laboratory than a home, considering the sterility of the environment. Everything that was painted was white, and the majority of the tables were stainless steel. A small corner was splashed with the brown of a couch, two recliners, and the reflection from an inactive video screen.

"Hard to believe that two murders happened in here." Rivka walked slowly through the area, looking at the outlines on the floor where each body had lain. "They didn't find a weapon."

"The case file was glaringly devoid, yes," Grainger said

as if answering a question. Rivka had been making a statement as she thought out loud. "Any thoughts, people?"

Chi walked through the area. "We've seen plenty of dead bodies in our day," he started as he examined the way the person had fallen. He looked at his datapad for pictures of the scene and studied the autopsy notes. And then he returned. "Their heads hit something."

"Of course their heads hit something," Jael said.

"What I mean is, as opposed to something hitting their heads. The momentum was generated by the head moving to impact a stationary object."

"Why didn't the autopsy say that?" Jael asked skeptically.

Rivka speculated on the answer. "This is a peaceful planet. They don't see these kinds of things here." She closed her eyes as she turned to face different parts of the room. In her mind's eye, she tried to recreate the events, imagining the bodies first and then moving backward through time. The timelines diverged rapidly.

"They weren't killed here," she said. Everyone nodded. The coroner had also noted that in his report. "Did someone carry the bodies through the hallways of the complex? I doubt it. Spread out," Rivka told them. "I've sent the three-dimensional image of the object or surface shaped like the wound."

The others accessed their datapads. Chi and Buster went upstairs. The others stayed on the first level. It didn't take long.

"Here," Chi called over the railing into the open area below. The Magistrates headed up the stairs with Lindy close behind. Red stayed in the apartment's open doorway, looking out, not in.

There was an office with desks upstairs, but only a single grossly oversized bed. Jael said what everyone was thinking. "That's pretty creepy."

Chi pointed to the decorations on the bed's footboard. "Could have been any one of those."

The four protrusions were round, about half the size of a human head. "Why didn't their investigators find this? It's almost a gimme."

"Peaceful planet. The investigators were probably distraught at seeing the violence. Look at us. We're immune to it."

Buster and Chi made big eyes at each other. "I've done far worse," Bustamove declared.

"Which of us hasn't?" Grainger asked softly. Even Rivka nodded slowly.

"Back to the crime. Are we certain that all five were in here?"

"Yes," Grainger replied.

"Then all three are complicit, no matter which one was pounding heads," Chi suggested.

"Odd that both would be in here and die in the same way. What's the chance of that? Suggests it was deliberate," Jael offered. She gave Rivka a broad smile.

"Teeth," Rivka said.

"What? I brushed."

"Not you. The perps. What if there's a senior clone? One who was made off-planet somewhere and then made the other four? That senior clone would be the one who would be guilty of cloning the others. They talk strangely, did you see that? They never showed their teeth, except that third one. He was more than happy to show his pearly whites. Back to the morgue."

The others followed Rivka as she hurried out. Grainger ordered the bus to stand by. Rivka started to run.

Red saw her coming and signaled for her to fall in behind him. He jogged slowly down the hallway.

"What's the rush?" Chi whispered.

"I don't know," Buster replied.

"It is kind of exciting, don't you think? Cracking the crime to mete out Justice!" Jael declared.

"That's what we do every day," Buster said.

"Not like this," Grainger admitted. "I would have already sent the three suspects to Jhiordaan. None of us do it like this, except for her."

"I like her way. Slower, but I like it." Jael nodded as she trotted after the big man carrying the railgun.

When they reached the bus, Rivka took the seat behind Red and hunched over her datapad. "Beau, please connect me to Doctor Toofakre on Federation Border Station 7."

A happy face appeared, his mask pulled down past his chin.

"Rivka! To what do I owe the pleasure? Or maybe I missed a lunch engagement, and you're going to arrest me." He looked alarmed, but only for a moment as Rivka chuckled.

"No. I need some dental forensics. Can you describe genetic conditions for teeth that would get fixed, but still could leave the same dental pattern?"

"You've come to the right man. To answer your question, yes."

She waited, but he didn't say anything else. She knew the image hadn't frozen because he blinked slowly and regularly.

"Well?"

"Well, what? I answered your question. Was there something else?"

"What are the genetic conditions?"

"As you have demonstrated, that is a completely different question. Precision in language, Magistrate, as you've lectured me." Tyler smiled but continued quickly after seeing the look on Rivka's face. "The first thing that comes to mind is *amelogenesis imperfecta.* The enamel doesn't form properly, resulting in teeth that are misshapen, stained brown, and often painful to the patient. They come in this way from birth due to a genetic abnormality."

"I suspect they weren't misshapen in a way that needed to be corrected since the dental patterns are identical in the five that we are examining."

"It's quite impossible for five people to have the exact same dental pattern," the dentist said, shaking his head.

"Not if they're identical clones, but only one had his teeth cleaned up, if I had to fathom a guess, and that would not have carried over to the others." Rivka looked somewhere else, already thinking ahead until Tyler waved from the screen to get her attention. "And consider this privileged information as part of an ongoing investigation. Tell no one or I'll have to kick your ass."

Doctor Toofakre's mouth opened, but she cut him off before he could speak. She looked up and smiled. "Got you."

Grainger met her gaze. "You owe him a nice dinner and maybe a short getaway on a pleasure moon somewhere."

"*What?*"

Red's head shook as he fought his laughter.

Jael enunciated each syllable. "*Plea*-sure moon."

"Fine. As soon as I retire from the Magistrates, I'll gallivant around the galaxy seeking personal gratification. Until then, *Justice*, bitches!"

Grainger leaned back to stare at her. "And you have the gall to call me strange."

It took no time at the morgue to confirm that the teeth of the two on the slab were discolored. They hopped back into the bus and headed for a final meeting with the senior jurist.

Red and Lindy handed over their gear without breaking stride on the way to the elevator. Two elevator trips found the five Magistrates and two bodyguards on the tenth floor, waiting for the senior jurist. She walked through a door beside the elevator.

"My office is one floor down. Those are the stairs," she said at Red's harsh look. He wished he'd known that for contingency planning purposes.

Everyone lies, he thought, *even if they simply don't tell the whole truth. What would it have hurt to tell me there were stairs?* Red's face worked through his frustration. Lindy noted her partner's angst and brushed against him, fondling a buttock where the others couldn't see. His upset faded and he winked at her.

"Please bring the three perps to one place so we can talk to them together," Rivka told her.

She pointed with her chin at the guards behind the glass. One hurried out as the other picked up a comm link.

"Where they did the brain scans. That will work. How did those turn out, by the way?" Pasifa asked.

"Inconclusive," Rivka replied, walking side by side with the senior jurist. "Everyone's thoughts are unique. In this case, similar, but unique. Also, each had put himself into a different emotional state to mess with the scan. The exercise as a whole was illuminating because it threw the suspects off their game."

"Interesting." When Rivka brushed her arm, she could feel that the older female was relieved by the impending resolution of the case. She wanted to return to her sedate life—the peaceful existence she embraced as the bedrock of her planet's culture. Rivka wanted to believe that such a place existed as much as the senior jurist, but the full holding cells suggested that Pass might have been living in her own dream world one floor below where she didn't have to see or hear the incarcerated.

Rivka moved away, looking at the floor as they walked, refusing to make eye contact with anyone as they walked by the cells. An arm reached out from a cell, trying to grab Jael. She grabbed and twisted, snapping the forearm without breaking stride. The perp started screaming. Pass hurried ahead.

"Keep your hands to yourself, asshole," Grainger mumbled before speaking more clearly. "You have been judged."

The room had been cleared of equipment. A table now

rested where the scan station had been. Six chairs kept the table company. None of the Magistrates sat down, but Rivka pulled one out for Pass to sit. She then put three chairs side by side against the back wall. It wasn't long before the three suspects arrived, their shackles and chains rattling softly.

Grainger pointed to the chairs. The three Gregars weaved amongst themselves to confuse those watching. No one tried to stop them. They took their seats, pleased with their deception.

Rivka took center stage. "Let's see your teeth." None of them opened their mouths.

"We can help," Buster offered. He, Chi, and Jael approached, each grabbing a suspect's face and peeling the lips back. The Gregars tried to bite the Magistrates, but that only earned them immediate punishment in the form of a knee to the chest or slap to the side of the head.

Only one had white teeth.

"Even a clone has a vain side. You were cloned from some long-gone original on a planet far away. You brought additional material here to create the others, but they weren't doing what you wanted or something like that. The reason you did it is unimportant. You were eliminating them one by one so you could start over. Of course they complied, because that is what they do. You are all clones and do as you're told. You have more free will, but that's because it is what you were told."

The clones looked confused.

"I have free will!" one stated. Rivka ignored him.

"The judgment is this: you, Gregar the original clone, are guilty of murder. You will be sent to Jhiordaan to live out the rest of your days. You two. Being a clone isn't illegal, but participating in a murder is. Your punishment as accomplices after the fact is that you will be surgically maimed so you can be told apart. You will then be exiled from Opheramin to separate corners of the galaxy where you will have no money, only low-paying manual labor positions. By the time you earn enough to leave your situation, you'll be old men. If you commit another crime, you'll expedite the meeting with your brother on Jhiordaan."

Rivka walked back and forth as she talked, never taking her eyes from the three clones. She stopped and faced them one last time.

"This judgment is final."

Rivka turned to walk away and the first Gregar tried to leap from his seat, but his shackles caught when he raised his hands to get the chain around her neck. Buster caught the chain running down his back and using his enhanced strength, pulled the clone back and slammed him into the wall.

Grainger tapped on his datapad. "Beau. You heard the judgment. Issue the orders." He nodded politely to Pasifa. "Thank you for your hospitality. We'll be leaving now."

Without further ado, Red led the way out, walking quickly since he'd had enough of Opheramin and clones.

They all had.

Grainger caught up with Rivka. "You weren't going to zombie him? You know, just to be sure?"

"I was one-hundred-percent sure. I didn't need to see into a warped mind to confirm what I already knew." Rivka slowed. "How are you ever certain enough to adjudicate a case?"

CHAPTER SEVEN

Collum Gate

First Minister Mol Gat strolled the promenade, his mane shining with the colors of the rainbow. As a single male from Alma Nine, he showed his hair in the way that peacocks did on Earth and for the same reason. He was trolling for mates. He was good with interspecies, being open to the adventurous side.

It never hurt one's chances of being an ambassador, either. His head held high, he window shopped, having no reason to be there except for the exercise and the fresh air. There weren't enough people around to make it a proper showing.

The capital city's shopping district was nearly a ghost town, but he wasn't afraid. He wanted to believe that he was showing the courage of his people. A couple ambassadors had died recently, but he chalked it up to random chance. The style of murder was different for each. He didn't think they were related.

Any place worth living had a certain level of excitement. Like the time he met Jack Marber, a fine example of what fearless looked like.

From a side alley, a beggar appeared. With nothing else to do, Mol Gat, feeling magnanimous, pulled a token credit chip from his pocket, a throwaway that he offered to the man. The female? Mol Gat couldn't tell since the individual was covered like a leper.

Which was probably for the best. The ambassador would have to take an anti-bacterial bath when he returned to his quarters, but for the moment, he would be kind and giving.

When the beggar was close enough to reach out and take the chip, he took another step closer. A gleaming, thin blade appeared in his hand, and he thrust. Mol Gat's eyes shot wide. The beggar twisted the blade, churning the ambassador's insides. When the attacker drew his hand back, the knife disappeared under the coverings.

With a casual turn, the beggar walked away.

No one saw the ambassador drop to his knees, mouth agape, dying. His mind screamed in terror, but his body wouldn't respond. He couldn't call for help. The credit chip fell to the ground, and the body of Alma Nine's ambassador followed.

Federation Border Station 7

After the frigate's return, the Magistrates had one final meeting.

"Thanks for parking in the hangar bay. I don't look good in an environmental suit," Jael said.

"Does anyone?" Rivka asked.

"I think Buzz Spacestar does, but I believe he's not in space with his," Chi claimed.

"The actor?" Rivka rolled her eyes and then her whole head while sticking her tongue out.

"Capture that image, Philko!" Buster stated. "Aha! Being named after an actor, I don't appreciate your tone when it comes to my fellows, so you shall pay, Rivka Anoa. I don't even have to manipulate this image."

"With friends like you..." Rivka left the remainder unsaid.

"With friends like me, we get to welcome a special guest traveling through. Everyone, say hello to Barnabas." Grainger looked at the door. He looked away, waited, and then pointed to the door.

"Say hello to Barnabas!" he repeated. When no one stepped through, the Magistrates stopped watching the door.

"Who is Barnabas?" Rivka asked, hoping to get a rise out of Grainger. He ignored the jibe. Of course, she knew who Barnabas was. She'd gone to law school on the QBBS *Meredith Reynolds.*

Grainger searched the Magistrate's conference room with his eyes as if someone were hiding. Once he declared the room clear, he explained, "Barnabas is Ranger One. Or rather, he was. He did not become a Magistrate, but he's on our side, scouring the universe with Shinigami."

"What's a Shinigami?"

"His AI, and his ship. All of it."

"I was supposed to intern with him when my training was completed, but we didn't quite get there," Buster lamented. "I've met him once, but that was right before the Rangers disbanded. I wanted to *be* him. He was the bomb!"

"A real bomb? Wouldn't he explode?" Jael taunted.

The door popped open, and a man with a pleasant smile on his face walked through it. He was of medium height, with light brown hair and blue eyes, and he was dressed anachronistically in a brown three-piece suit, the jacket off and dangling from his fingertips.

He closed the door carefully behind him. The Magistrates were already standing. Buster pushed past Grainger to pump the Ranger's hand, and Barnabas laughed easily as he greeted the other man. He glanced around the room, resting his eyes briefly on one person before moving to another.

"Please, take a seat and share some words of wisdom," Grainger offered.

He nodded but shook each person's hand. When he shook Rivka's hand, she didn't *want* to see into his mind, but a couple of emotions flashed through. He was worried. She saw a strange image: what looked like a glass jar with a jellyfish inside, and someone in a long cloak. She frowned. What was Barnabas investigating?

He winked at her. He could read minds, too, and could do it without having to touch the person. He knew that Rivka knew, but he didn't let it bother him.

Barnabas took a seat and kicked back, beaming a smile at the group. "Words of wisdom. Hmm." He looked at the ceiling and considered. "Well, you'll have an idea about the missions, but no one tells you the shit you'll be putting up with from everyone else—bureaucrats, low-level station administrators, bankers. And during the past few missions,

I've had a crew of gloriously incompetent pirates trying to steal my ship."

"Talk to us about your current mission. I sense it's bothering you. Maybe we can help. We have some resources," Rivka politely suggested. Grainger studied her, wondering what she had seen.

Barnabas gave her an intrigued look before settling back in his seat. "Ah. I suppose I could do that. We responded to a distress call from a civilian ship. Now, this was far out—well out of Federation territory. They know of humans there, but not well, and there are a few species you might not know: Brakalons, Ubuara, Luvendi, Jotun."

The group all leaned forward to listen, eager to hear more.

"A Jotun was murdered on the transport," Barnabas explained. "Now, the Jotun are—well, they sort of look like jellyfish, so what they do is they make these mechanical suits that have a tank in the middle of them. They kind of float there and control the suit with their tentacles."

"That's crazy," Buster whispered.

"No, what's crazy is trying to tell them apart." Barnabas flashed him a smile. "Anyway, the ship had to be brought to a halt because under Brakalon law, if a crime happens on a spaceship, you have to stop the whole thing and wait for authorities to arrive. Well…there was a complication."

"Isn't there always," Grainger muttered.

Barnabas gave a low laugh. "Every single time, I swear. So, the first thing that happened was we showed up, and there was a spaceship a little ways away from the *Srisa*, trying to block the distress signal and shooting down any ship that tried to approach."

The group looked at each other, intrigued by this development.

"It was an advanced craft, and probably would have taken down any other ship easily, but—well, the *Shinigami* was Bethany Anne's personal ship." Barnabas gave a small, self-satisfied smile. "It was easy to evade what this ship was throwing at us and tail them. We figured we'd be able to unravel the murder easily, except that the alien flying it used a self-destruct protocol rather than talk to us."

"Over a single murder?" Rivka demanded. "Who was this person?"

"Interesting question. I assume you mean the murdered Jotun, yes?" Barnabas waited for her nod. "Yes, he was a ship captain in the Jotun Navy. Now, something you probably won't know—I worked with the Jotun Navy on my last mission, and that was against the direct orders of their Senate. Long story short, we were going up against a corporation that had bribed some of the senators to look the other way, and the Navy wasn't willing to. One of our best theories is that the murdered captain helped in the battle, and the Senate had him killed. But there are some issues with that theory."

"They'd have publicized it if they did, wouldn't they?" Rivka pointed out. "Because they'd want it to be a warning, right? Or a very public punishment, at least."

"That's a good point." Barnabas frowned. "Also strange is the fact that the other ship waited by the *Srisa*. They didn't take the actual assassin and leave, and the assassin didn't shut down the *Srisa's* distress signal. It's as if the two weren't working together—but both of them wanted what they were doing to be kept quiet."

Grainger sat back and rubbed his chin in thought.

"Well, he was involved in *something* shady," Buster said finally. He shrugged and looked around at the others. "Right? He had to be. He screwed someone over hard, probably with someone else. The assassin killed him quietly—"

"Why, though?" Rivka interrupted.

"I don't know, but let me finish. So they killed him quietly, and the other ship was there because his accomplices suspected that was why he was killed, and they didn't want anyone to find out about it. They were going to try to hush it up, you know?"

Barnabas was staring at him, frowning slightly. An idea was clearly coming to him. "They sent a message to the Jotun government," he said slowly. "The captain of the *Srisa* said he had sent a message. I assumed it was to the Navy—but what if he sent it to the Senate?"

Buster gave him a deer-in-the-headlights look. "I'm not sure I quite—"

"We all thought he was assassinated by the Senate for helping the Navy," Barnabas explained. "But what if he was assassinated by the Navy for helping the Senate?" He slapped his leg. "That's it. That's absolutely it. They sent that ship to keep anyone from investigating until their own people could get to it. Oh, Jeltor is not going to be happy." He rubbed his face and stood. "I...have to go right now, I'm afraid. There are some people I need to talk to before any more assassins get hired. Thank you all." He ran for the doorway and pelted through it, only to stick his head back around the doorframe a moment later. "It was very nice to meet all of you. I hope we'll meet again, and if you're ever in need of aid, do call on the *Shinigami*."

He left, footsteps receding at high speed.

"He's a lot more old-fashioned than I expected," Buster said finally.

"He was a monk on Earth," Grainger said.

The others stared at him, mouths hanging open.

"You're kidding," Buster said.

"Nuh-uh." Grainger shook his head. "His manners were kind of an inside joke amongst the rest of the Rangers. They all said he had a stick up his ass, but he'd do anything for his allies."

Grainger scrolled through a number of screens. "We are in an enviable position in that there are more cases than we can adjudicate. So, for the first time ever, you have some say in which missions you'll go on."

"I like the new Grainger!" Rivka declared.

"New feathers on our shiny bird. Well done, Magistrate!" Jael added.

"First up, Buster, I'll need you to investigate spaceships crashing on Parkilo Prime. We've had two Federation vessels and one private ship crash on their final approach. Something is going on, and it's a Federation issue."

"Whoa! What happened to choosing our missions?" Buster complained.

"As soon as I heard the words out loud, the whole thing sounded wrong, so I changed my mind."

Jael raised one hand, and with the other, she cranked as

if using a fishing pole. Her middle finger slowly raised until it was the sole upright digit.

Rivka revised her position. "I *don't* like the new Grainger."

"Moving on!" He smiled at the Magistrates. "Chi and Jael—"

"Wait a minute," Buster interrupted, looking at his data-pad. "Parkilo Prime is populated by sentient plants?"

"Yes. Sentient plants with a big problem. They need you, Bustamove. They need you to work your Magistrate magic and resolve their issue. I picked you because there's probably a cyber component to the crime. It doesn't answer the question of why, but may lead you to who. So there you are."

Buster wanted to argue, but it made sense. His AI Philko appreciated a challenge.

"Chi, I need you to dig into the pits of something called the Damu Michezo on the planet Tol. With their application for membership to the Federation approved, we need to validate that this death match bullshit isn't being corrupted within Federation Law. Someone called Valerie conducted an interdiction there once. You need to see if they still understand."

Chi pointed to Rivka. "Sounds perfect for Zombie," he deflected. She didn't agree.

"No, it's all you, my man. Dig in and see how they run it. I hear the Skulla are something else, so good luck with all that. We need a fighter on this one who will have some credibility. She looks like a strong breeze could blow her over." Grainger pointed with a thumb.

"Hey! I resemble that remark," Rivka quipped. She was

taller and heavier than when she had first joined the Magistrates thanks to the Pod-doc, but she hadn't gained as much as Lindy.

"Jael..."

"Why am I always last?" Rivka wondered.

Grainger ignored her. "Jael, you get voter interference on the frontier planet of Jurdenia." He tapped his screen to send her the file. She gave him her best stunned-mullet face.

Rivka slid down in her seat until her eyeballs peeked over the edge of the table.

"And Rivka gets the icing on the cake." Grainger paused for dramatic effect, but the Magistrates were making faces as they looked at the files. He had to stretch upward to make eye contact with Rivka. "Fine. This one is a bit disconcerting. It appears that someone is executing alien ambassadors on the planet of Collum Gate. This place held promise as a hub for intersystem negotiation. Even Yoll has taken advantage of the opportunity to negotiate boundary issues. It's raising tensions amongst all the alien representatives since everyone assumes it's one of them doing it."

"A serial killer or a starter of wars?" Rivka considered while sitting up in her seat. "I'll take it."

She started digging into the case file Grainger had released to her. The others disappeared into the background as she focused on the information.

Rivka jumped up, startling the others. "I need to go. See you after we save the day." She bolted from the room, yelling at her datapad for Chaz to recall the crew.

The Magistrate hurried aboard *Peacekeeper*. Red remained outside the corvette, waiting on his better half.

Lindy had been out running errands, since only one of the bodyguards had been needed while Grainger's meeting was ongoing. She was on her way.

"Chaz, what's the status of the crew?" Rivka asked.

"Ankh and Erasmus are in their laboratory. Lindy is on her way. I haven't been able to contact Jay, but her embedded comm chip says that she is in the spa."

"Again?" Rivka chuckled as she rushed back to the hatch. "Red, can you have Lindy stop by the spa and drag Jay out of there? I'm sorry, I mean, 'coordinate her immediate departure.'"

Red put a finger to his temple as he activated his comm chip to talk with Lindy. A moment later he replied, "She's on her way. She will coordinate Jay's immediate departure, even if that means Lindy has to throw her over a shoulder and carry her."

"They've called five times, Mistress Jayita. I think you should talk to them."

"Nopity nope," Jay mumbled into her towel as the four-handed alien continued to work on her back. The Pod-doc process had added weight, girth, and height. Lindy chose to deal with the changes by working out to excess. Jay decided there would be plenty of time for that later, so she turned to pampering.

A commotion outside the massage studio signaled the end of Jay's reverie.

The door opened none too gently. "There you are!" Lindy declared. "We have to go. Immediate mission. Need to save the universe. Chop chop."

Lindy crossed her arms and motioned with her eyeballs that it was time to get up.

"Get out," Lindy told the masseuse. "Please."

Jay groaned and whined as she got dressed. "We sit around forever, and then all of a sudden we're in a hurry. What is up with that? Has being deliberate gone out of vogue?"

"If only the criminals would cooperate. And we haven't been sitting around. We've only been back on station for what, six hours?"

"Not me." Jay pulled on a new blouse, loose to hang over her yoga pants. On their way out, an older woman stopped them.

"I'm sorry, but your credit chip has been rejected." The woman was standing between them and the door. Lindy wanted to go but wouldn't leave her friend hanging.

"What's the damage?" she asked.

"Nearly ten thousand credits."

Lindy's lips turned white, and she clenched her teeth, glaring at Jay. The younger woman, who was sporting platinum-blue hair, smiled weakly. "I've never looked at prices before..." she started to say.

"Now's a good time to start!" Lindy stated angrily.

"I believe I have seven thousand." Jay handed her personal chip to the older woman, who withdrew the maximum it would allow.

"You still owe two-thousand eight hundred credits."

Lindy pulled out her chip and held it out. The older

woman ran the charge, beaming after it went through. "Add your usual tip?"

Before Lindy could answer, Jay spoke. "Of course."

The average person did everything they could to avoid confrontation. The relief on the older woman's face was clear that she was happy that the situation was resolved with minimal grief.

Lindy took the chip and shoved it back into her pocket. She made growling noises deep in her throat.

"I'm sorry. I'll pay you back."

Lindy turned on her. "I just paid three thousand credits at a spa, and I didn't get a single knot massaged out. You'll take care of that when we're on board!"

"Done!" Jay continued to profusely thank Lindy for saving her from the embarrassment of not being able to leave the spa.

"I still can't believe you spent ten grand on the spa. How long have you been in there?"

"When did we get back?"

"Two weeks ago. You've been in the spa that whole time?"

"Not the *whole* time," Jay stammered. "Well. The Poddoc and then some shopping, but outside of that, yes. I've been here."

"I don't know what to say." Jay kept falling back. "Keep up, we're in a hurry."

"My legs are a little rubbery," she tried to explain.

"Two solid weeks of massages. No shit, your legs are rubbery. You're working out starting about five seconds after the *Peacekeeper's* hatch closes."

"You used to be so much more fun," Jay grumbled.

"I used to be three grand richer, too."

Rivka sat on the bridge and scrolled through the case file. She pored over every word. Three ambassadors had died, one was lost with his entire entourage. Seven victims in total. Each attack had been unique. Besides the fact that an ambassador had been killed, there was nothing linking the deaths. None of them had been working on similar projects. There was no overlap. There was nothing that jumped out at her screaming, "Start here!"

She thought she heard the ship's engines start and felt a gentle bump as *Peacekeeper* lifted off the deck on its way out of the docking bay.

"Status," she requested.

"We are leaving the station on our way to clear space, where we'll activate the Gate engines and jump to Collum Gate. Systems and stores are one hundred percent."

"Thanks, Chaz." Rivka stood and stretched. She needed a good night's sleep if she were to tackle the fineries of the diplomatic circuit. "Call the crew to the rec room for a quick catch-up."

"All hands, all hands, mandatory meeting in *Peacekeeper*'s nerve center, right now!" Chaz blasted through the ship's systems.

"I think I should have been clear that you weren't to shake everyone out of their skin," Rivka clarified a few moments too late.

"My bad, Magistrate," the EI whispered.

The hatch opened, and she left the bridge. Four steps

later she walked into the rec room, where no one looked happy.

"Sorry about that. Chaz is overly excited to be back on the job." No one smiled. "Okay. Out with it."

Lindy pointed at Jay.

"Jay?" Rivka demanded.

"My parents cut me off."

"Why is that a surprise? You're supposed to be in jail," Rivka shot back.

"But. Well. I was spending money like I always do..." She hesitated. Lindy crossed her arms and tapped her foot. "Lindy had to bail me out of the spa."

"You were incarcerated in the spa? Is that a thing?" Rivka was confused.

Jay hung her head, her face flushed.

"She ran up a ten-grand tab."

"That's a lot of body oil," Rivka surmised. "And man candy."

"I had to borrow money from Lindy!" she blurted. "I'm so sorry." Jay started sobbing.

"It's just money," Rivka offered. Lindy turned into Red's embrace, and he held her tightly.

Ankh watched emotionlessly. "I can take care of that if you'd like."

"Would you?" Jay asked. Rivka was skeptical, unsure what Ankh meant. His eyes glazed as he communed with the AI resident in his head and together, they tapped through the networks.

"Lindy's money has been restored to her chip, as has yours. The initial charge was unlocked and covered by the original chip," he claimed.

"My parents allowed the charge?" Jay smiled through her tears. He didn't dignify her question with an answer.

Rivka glared at Ankh. "We use our superpowers for good, Ankh," Rivka said. "Put it all back the way it was, please."

He disappeared into his own world for a few moments before his eyes cleared, and he met Rivka's gaze. "It is undone, except for Lindy's payment. There is a loan in Jay's name which she will pay back from her wages as part of your crew."

"Ankh! That was a very decent thing for you to do. And legal, for what it's worth." Rivka nodded once. She would have hugged him, but the Crenellian was even less touchy-feely than Red. "Thank you."

Jay was oblivious to the huggability of others. She threw herself on Ankh and hugged him to her, picking him up and swinging him around before setting him back down and apologizing. She picked him back up for one more long hug. She set him down again and sat, closing her eyes as she took deep and slow breaths.

"Don't do that," Ankh told her in his small voice.

Lindy started to reach for him, but Red stopped her. He suspected the Crenellian regarded hugs as a form of torture. It probably took all he had to tell Jay not to do it.

The air grew thick, and no one spoke. It was Rivka's ship, her crew, and her responsibility to keep the peace.

"We have a tough case coming up," Rivka said firmly, pointing to the screen where Chaz had brought up the case file. "Ambassadors are being murdered. The Federation wants this one brought to a conclusion sooner rather than later. Seven deaths, three of them ambassadors, in the past week. Someone is knocking off alien dignitaries, and we can't have that. I'm afraid that no matter how quickly we get there and start working the case, the bodies will continue to pile up. Some worlds have already evacuated their staffs.

"Do you hear those words as I do? *Evacuate*, as if Collum Gate were a war zone. What makes this case so important is that Collum Gate has been growing as one of the best places in the galaxy for alien worlds to negotiate. Many treaties have been signed there because the various parties can negotiate in peace. If we lose that, the Federation doesn't know if it can be replaced. The sentient species of this galaxy could stop talking. If that happens, we all lose."

"What you're saying is that you have another intergalactic war to stop before it starts, you and the four of us. Seven, if you count that cat and the AIs." Red rubbed his chin after being so profound.

"Something like that. For the record, I don't count Hamlet."

"Don't count him out," Jay joked, having recovered some of her composure.

"There's the case file if you want to look at it. Pull up a map of the embassies, Chaz, so Red can get the lay of the land. We'll meet with local law enforcement and Dignitary Security as soon as we land. In the meantime, I need some sleep." Rivka started to walk toward her cabin. "Chaz. Take us in, but hold orbit until after I've had a good eight hours of sleep."

"How do I evaluate if you have had a good sleep, Magistrate?" Chaz asked.

"How about you hold station until I tell you?"

"I can do that. Sleep fast, Magistrate."

Rivka nodded toward Red and Lindy. "Keep the peace in my absence. And the quiet. Yes, peace and quiet."

Red started talking to the ceiling. "Chaz, prepare the room for physical training. Jay, you have some iron to throw."

CHAPTER EIGHT

"No!" Rivka declared, putting her foot down to emphasize her denial.

Red leaned toward her with his hands out, pleading. "Let us take the mech. You won't even know it's there." He smiled pleasantly while Lindy made faces behind him.

"You know we can't show up with a mech. You think that we'll take fire and you don't want anything to happen to Lindy." Rivka struck a nerve; Red winced. Lindy punched him in the back.

"I'll take care of myself. We'll be wearing full ballistic protection, but you are not going to treat me differently. Didn't we already have this protective man conversation?"

Red bit his lip while competing emotions warred within. Lindy hugged him from behind and apologized softly.

Rivka gave him a moment before continuing, "We are going in heavy, but not with a mech. I'm sorry Red, but we have a job to do that doesn't include increasing the fear. We walk in confidently. We find the fucker who's doing this, and then we deliver the judgment. If we are getting into firefights, we'll unstrap the mech, and we'll go to war. Until then, heads on a swivel and stay out of the open."

The mech suit was strapped conspicuously on top of *Peacekeeper*. Getting into it would be problematic at the best of times, but there was no room for it inside the ship. Red had hoped to either maneuver it into the cargo bay while in space or climb into it while the ship was on the ground. In either case, it would take time and wasn't something that could be done while under fire.

As the head of security, Red was challenged to know when they needed to man the suit before they came under fire. Their track record in regard to acting versus reacting wasn't stellar.

"When we need to put on the suit, we won't be able to delay," he argued.

"I think when we need support from a mech, it will be patently obvious."

"And probably too late," Red retorted.

"And that is the razor's edge that we will have to walk," Rivka replied. "I understand, big guy. I like knowing your firepower has my back. I like knowing that Lindy's firepower has yours. With Jay, we have four sets of eyes watching. That has to be better than when it was just us, doesn't it?" Rivka tried to explain.

"You have me, too. I shall come with you," the Crenellian stated, his voice even and emotionless.

"I'm not sure about that, Ankh."

"It is logical. I'm the only so-called alien member of the crew. I'm the only one who can tap into security feeds wherever we may be, and I'm the only one who doesn't come across as threatening."

The others moved aside to let Ankh into their circle. Red looked over Ankh's head at Jay. The small alien with the big head knew what the large bodyguard was implying.

"She's terrifying," Ankh whispered.

Rivka coughed and turned away, covering her face. She choked until she headed for the small galley to get a drink of water. "Thanks for reprogramming the food thing," she said after downing a glass and ordering a food bar. "This stuff is edible now."

Ankh looked at her but didn't reply.

"Can you program Grainger's ship to produce only borscht-flavored bars?" she asked.

"Of course," he replied. "If I knew what borscht was."

"Never mind, then. It was a random thought. I need to focus on what we're doing. I see this as a chess match. The murderer—and for now, I'm assuming that we have one perp and not a strange coincidence—has already made at least three moves, maybe more. We're playing catch up. This person likes to kill high-profile aliens. Does Crenellia have a diplomatic presence here?"

Ankh considered the question. An emotion briefly crossed his features, something they'd not seen before and couldn't relate to a human response.

"A diplomatic presence, no," he finally answered.

"We may need you to play the Crenellian ambassador, Ankh."

"I am not the ambassador," he related the fact.

"As the only Crenellian here, there's no reason why you

can't be." Rivka smiled as a plan started to take shape in her mind.

"My people already have a presence here, but not an ambassador. I cannot speak for Crenellia."

"Crenellians are here, but there's no embassy?"

"There is a vehicle waiting outside for the crew of *Peacekeeper*," Chaz reported.

"They'll have to wait. Chaz, bring up everything you can find on the Crenellians on Collum Gate."

The crew retreated to the middle of the recreation room. The five of them watched as a logo appeared on the screen followed by a short video ad. Company information scrolled by. Rivka shook her head.

"The Crenellians are arms dealers?"

"My people sell defensive weaponry, yes."

"That looked like a hell of a lot more than defensive weapons," Red mumbled.

"Some of the weaponry has an offensive component, but the market is huge for planets only wishing to protect themselves from an alien invasion."

"I'm glad you're on our team. Chaz, arrange a meeting with the Crenellians, too. We may need them to agree to give Ankh the title of ambassador." Rivka signaled that it was time to leave. "Jay? You've been awfully quiet. We need your powers of perception. As a member of the crew, it's time to earn your keep."

"I'm so sore!" she blurted.

"What did you do?" Rivka demanded of Red and Lindy.

"Worked out, like she should have done since the Pod-doc finished with her. We have a lot of ground to make up," Lindy explained.

"Okay," Rivka replied pleasantly. "Put on your walking shoes, Jay. We're going to town."

Opulence greeted the crew when they left the ship. The vehicle took them to a welcome terminal where they were treated to a wide a variety of sights and smells, a representative sampling of the galaxy-wide treats brought to Collum Gate to make any traveler feel welcome. Red walked in front carrying his railgun, and at the back of the entourage, Lindy carried hers. She found that she could look over Rivka's head, now that she'd been through two sessions in the Pod-doc.

Lindy liked her physical changes. The added four inches of height gave her a completely different perspective. And she could carry weight she had previously considered unfathomable. She told Rivka that if Red went down again, she could carry him. The Magistrate was good with that. Red promised them both for that to happen again, they'd be carrying his corpse.

Jay wanted to stop and browse a couple of the small shops in the massive corridor that welcomed new arrivals.

"We need to get to work, but it'll be here when we leave. I hope that the people will have an upbeat attitude then because their world will be safe once more." As they passed, Rivka smiled and nodded at the shopkeepers.

"These folks are anxious because it's their livelihood that's being threatened," Jay replied. "There's no threat to their lives, just their health and well-being."

"I think that's the same thing," Rivka said.

Ankh walked along casually. The Magistrate had to slow down since he was already breathing heavily. Red slowed down without looking after Lindy informed him of the pace using the embedded comm chip. They maintained a running conversation while they evaluated threats and the ever-changing tactical situation. Red was in his element and being able to talk about what he did while doing it made him sharper.

And gave him an extra set of eyes, so he didn't have to turn around to see where the Magistrate was. He was responsible for one-hundred eighty degrees, not three-sixty. What mattered most to him was doing his job, keeping the Magistrate safe so she could do hers.

Someone almost ran into him with a cart. He hadn't seen it coming because he had let his mind wander.

Get your head out of your ass! he ordered himself, forcing his eyes back and forth to reestablish his situational awareness.

He held up his hand to stop the parade before the team exited. Rivka took the opportunity to look back at the decorations, which were bright without being gaudy. It was classy and well-manicured, a nice way to welcome dignitaries to Collum Gate.

Rivka snarled. And someone out there was ruining it for everyone.

She pulled Ankh close. Chaz had already notified authorities of the Crenellian ambassador's arrival, so the bait had already been dangled. She was still wrestling with whether to meet with the Crenellians first as part of the ploy or start the investigation. The warrior in her won out. Law enforcement called to her.

Red waved the group forward once he made eye contact with their hover-van driver.

"Stay close," he called over his shoulder. He led the way down broad steps, in the classic style of gleaming white marble.

Jay nodded appreciatively at the style and class. "I like the way they do things around here."

"How could you not?" Rivka agreed.

Fury!

The emotion hit her as if the person were standing next to her, but there was no one nearby. Why the anger, and at whom? Rivka wondered, throwing a protective arm around the Crenellian. He tried to shrug it off, but she pulled him closer and spun him around to face her.

A bullet raced through the space where he'd just been and tore into the Magistrate's abdomen. She doubled over and fell, rolling two steps before stopping and leaving a bloody smear behind.

"Get them in the van!" Red yelled. He leveled his railgun, but had no idea where the bullet had come from. The hiss of its passing left only the vaguest impression of its trajectory.

Lindy wanted to shoot something, but that wasn't her role. She slung her railgun over her shoulder and scooped up the Magistrate in one arm and Ankh in the other as she zigzagged her way down the remaining steps. Red remained where he was watching for any indication of another shot. A second bullet shattered marble behind Lindy's erratic path, and then she was in the van, pushing the others to the floor and lying on top of them.

Jay screamed and darted toward the van.

"Get in!" Red yelled at the driver as he ran. He still had no idea where either shot had come from, and that didn't matter.

The Magistrate was down.

Red jumped into the front passenger seat, and the driver shot off into traffic with wide eyes as he watched the travel lanes. He was trying not to think about the bleeding dignitary in the back.

"How is she?" Red managed to say over his shoulder, watching the outskirts of Collum Gate shoot by as they headed toward the city center.

"Should I go to the hospital, sir?" the driver asked in a shaky voice.

"She's coming around," Lindy replied after she lifted herself off the Crenellian and the Magistrate.

"I hate getting shot," she muttered. "Are we clear?"

"We're out of the ambush area," Red proclaimed. "We're clear if he, she, or it was working alone."

"Help me up." Lindy boosted Rivka into the seat, picked Ankh off the floor and put him next to her. Lindy kneeled on the floor to examine both. The Crenellian looked uninjured, albeit ruffled.

Rivka made faces and groaned as she reached inside her jacket. She winced as she removed her hand, then smiled. "Ha! Missed my datapad."

Red turned to the driver. "Take us to the law enforcement center. The cop shop. We need to have a word about the Magistrate's security."

"They weren't shooting at me. I only got in the way. Congratulations, Ambassador Ankh'Po'Turn. You are the first to survive a Collum assassination attempt. Maybe you and Erasmus can track the digital footprints to see who might have received the notice of your arrival?"

Ankh stared straight ahead and quickly became lost within his mind as he and Erasmus interfaced with the systems they needed to help them in their search.

"Would you look at this shit?" Rivka exclaimed, sounding stronger with each new word. "I have holes in my jacket!"

"You have holes in your body, too," Lindy said, unused to seeing wounded people. "I hope I never grow accustomed to this."

"Just enough to not let it bother you. It'll help you stay on the edge," Rivka told her. "Did you see where the shots came from?"

"I got nothing," she replied. "I never saw a puff of smoke, a distortion in the air, or a flash, and the sound seemed to come from multiple directions."

"Like a railgun but not, or the Magistrate would have been blown in half instead of that baby-sized hole she has," Red offered.

She pulled her shirt up to verify that the nanocytes had ejected the bullet and sealed the hole. "Baby-sized. Right." Rivka thought it had felt like a cannonball tearing through her body. "Damn, that hurt," she complained.

"We have to get lucky every time. They only have to get lucky once," Red said, knowing that he could influence the Magistrate's luck in most cases.

"Do you have any nanocytes, Ankh?"

The Crenellian didn't answer since he was deep within the cyber world.

"I don't think so," Rivka answered for him.

The driver kept glancing over his shoulder at the person they'd carried bleeding into his van. If there hadn't been a puddle of blood on the floor, he wouldn't have believed she'd been shot. Color had returned to her face, and she was talking as if nothing had happened.

"There's a big difference between a single trip to the Pod-doc and multiple trips to boost the little buggers within," she proclaimed. "You've had two?"

"Yes," Lindy replied simply.

"Red?"

"Three," he replied.

"Jay?"

The young woman was hunched over and spoke in a small voice. "One."

"You know what you're saying, don't you?" Rivka cautioned. "If you got shot like this, it would hurt more and take longer to heal. As soon as we get back, into the Pod-doc for rounds two and three, understand?"

"Yes, Magistrate," she replied as she continued to stare at the blood puddle on the van's floor.

"This person has pissed me off, Red. I don't like being pissed off. I feel compelled to do something about it."

Red nodded. "I'm not sure how well I can protect you," the big man said. "I thought we had it covered, and they still got a shot past me. How long did they have to set up the ambush? Minutes?"

"Every dignitary comes through that entry. Maybe Ankh was a target of opportunity, and the ambush had been set up for a long time. What better way to say you don't want war than to attack those who supply the arms?"

"That makes more sense than them being able to set up

something like that with no lead time. They had the perfect angle. I want this person as badly as you do, Magistrate. I can't abide someone making me look bad. I take my job seriously. We have yet to complete a mission where someone doesn't get hurt. You may have to fire me." Red was grumbling.

"There will be no reward by firing. You're going to suffer with the rest of us!" Rivka followed her statement with her best maniacal laugh.

"Does it take getting shot to put you in a good mood?" Lindy asked.

"It takes surviving to put me in a good mood. We'll get this nut grabber, make no mistake. There will be a judgment, and there will be an execution. I'll zombie every being in this city if I have to to find this person."

CHAPTER NINE

The hover-van pulled up in front of the law enforcement station, but Rivka told the driver to continue around the corner. She directed him, as per Chaz's instructions, into an enclosed area behind the building. When the driver finally parked, uniformed locals were waiting.

The driver seemed relieved to finally stop. He was the first one out and started walking in circles. Red ignored him, climbing out next to introduce himself to the officers. They looked at him and his railgun suspiciously until he slid the weapon around to his back and offered a hand.

He towered over the natives of Collum Gate. It was a slightly heavier gravity than Red was used to, which tended to make the locals shorter and squatter.

Lindy popped the side door and stepped out. She was covered in blood, as was Rivka. With her coat open, it looked like the bottom half of her shirt had been painted red. It still glistened with the freshness of undried blood.

With a determined stride, Rivka approached the group. The officers hurried to help the Magistrate, but she waved them off. Lindy watched from next to the van, her appearance one of guarded mirth. She gave Ankh a hand so he could get out. Jay stayed close to the Crenellian although he tried to edge away from her.

The driver staggered away from the hover-van, doubled over, and puked.

"What happened?" an older Collum officer asked.

"I'm Magistrate Rivka Anoa, and someone tried to kill my friend." She nodded toward the Crenellian.

The officer blew out a long breath. "No one was killed? Who was injured?" The other locals spread out to form a cordon around Rivka and her group.

Rivka pointed to herself.

"Call an ambulance!" he shouted over his shoulder.

"Stop!" Rivka ordered in her best Magistrate voice.

"No need," Red added. "Just a flesh wound, and it's been taken care of."

"The reception was unexpected only in how quickly it happened. I feel the pain of your investigation." Rivka looked at her shirt before turning toward Lindy. Her darker clothes made the blood stains less obvious. "I could use a new shirt, and then we need to talk about some things. Most importantly, our next steps."

"Let's go inside," the officer replied. "I'm Supra Harpeth, in charge of the investigation into the ambassadors' murders."

"I think that's why they were taking potshots. He's the Crenellian ambassador," Rivka told him, pointing with her thumb over her shoulder.

"We didn't know. So the attack was another on an ambassador? I better send my investigators to the scene of the attack based on this revelation. That was *you,* then."

"Yes. Coming down the front steps. I have to say that the welcome hall of the spaceport is second to none. I am impressed."

"Besides the shooting," Jay suggested.

Rivka shrugged noncommittally. "Besides the shooting, that is," she parroted. "We need to put a stop to whoever is doing this. I wouldn't be surprised to see all traffic through your arrivals terminal grind to a halt."

Supra Harpeth nodded to Rivka and bowed to Ankh. "Welcome to Collum Gate. I hope the unfortunate coincidence of a shooting at the spaceport doesn't prevent you from enjoying our lovely city."

"*Coincidence?*" Rivka wasn't sure she'd heard correctly. "I thought you were certain these were linked."

"We have no evidence that they are linked. They are each so different. One who shoots or bombs has a different mentality than one who is willing to look a victim in the face as they stab them."

The group started walking. The supra looked troubled. Rivka had told herself she was willing to use all her tools to solve this crime. No one outside the Magistrate's purview. She gently touched the supra's arm.

"I understand how disconcerting this could be. The entirety of Collum Gate's future is on your shoulders. You're the scapegoat, but know that we're here to solve this crime, stop the perp cold, and restore the security of those who live here. We'll get there," she said in a calm and even voice, all the while listening to the turmoil boiling within him.

He considered himself a failure because he'd had to call for help, but he had no leads and no suspects.

"We may have a lead," she offered. Hope sprang to his mind before she let go of his arm. "We'll need your conference room and a little time. We didn't want to start anything without you."

Red watched the exchange, relaxing while they walked through the station.

They had started their investigation the second they'd published the notification that Ankh was the ambassador. They'd gone fishing and had gotten a big bite. Red hoped Ankh would be able to trace the perps through cyberspace. He'd seen Ankh in action and was confident that if it could be done, the Crenellian and the AI who shared his head would be able to do it.

Jay tried to take Ankh's hand as if she were walking with a child, but he wouldn't let her, finally angling away until Lindy was between them.

"What's up, little man?" Jay asked.

"He's afraid of you," Lindy suggested without looking at Jayita.

"How so?"

"You're the serial hugger," Lindy chided.

"A title that I'm proud to carry, I'll have you know." Jay leaned around Lindy and waved her fingers at the Crenellian. He stiffened and kept looking forward.

"We have a great deal to talk about. Ankh? Do you have anything yet on how the information regarding the Crenellian Ambassador went astray?"

"I believe so," Ankh said less confidently than Rivka had hoped.

The screen shimmered to life as the supra stood there, waiting patiently for the media to drive the presentation. An image appeared on the screen, and a voice started talking using the system's speakers.

"Who's doing that?" Supra Harpeth asked.

The presentation froze. Rivka pointed to Ankh.

"How?" the supra continued.

"He's really smart," Rivka answered, leaving it at that. She twirled her finger in the air, and the presentation continued.

"The secret announcement regarding the arrival of the Crenellian was made at this point in time. The communication traveled within a fixed channel until here, when the signal was separated three ways. Two were official, and the third was an official-looking channel. Once the signal traveled into the secure systems, it was controlled. We are only interested in this third channel. It funneled the signal through a decoding system and then broadcast it. Once broadcast, we could not track the recipients."

"That isn't much of a lead, but it's more than *we* have," the supra admitted.

"It's not as much as we'll have once we tap the server. You'll need to visit the server farm, where I suspect you will find our next clue. I'm counting on it," Erasmus confirmed.

"Who was that?"

"Erasmus. One of Plato's stepchildren. An Artificial Intelligence."

"Where is it?"

"Erasmus? He's in Ankh's head," Rivka explained, growing perturbed at questions that wouldn't help them find a killer.

"The little guy is an AI?"

"No. Ankh is a Crenellian. The AI lives in his head with him, and he's sitting right here."

"That's really weird."

"You know what's weird? Us sitting around, talking about things that don't matter, when there's a server farm out there we need to raid." Rivka turned to Ankh. "Thank you, Ankh and Erasmus. If you'll give us the address, we'll get on our way."

"I'll get the armed response unit ready to go," Supra Harpeth stated. "And while they're getting ready, we'll contact the judge to get an access permit."

"We don't need an armed response unit, and we don't need an access permit. I'm a Magistrate. I issue my own warrants, and the shooter isn't at the server farm, is he, Ankh?" The Crenellian shook his head slightly. "There may be some security, but we can handle them. The fewer locals we put into the line of fire, the better off everyone will be. You are more than welcome to tag along."

"But, that's not how we do things on Collum Gate. We have protocols," the supra stammered.

"Federation Law supersedes. I'm sorry, but you no longer have jurisdiction. The Federation needs this case resolved, and quickly. I cannot overstate the importance of Collum Gate to the health and well-being of the Federation. Be proud of that. I want your help, but I call the shots. If you can't agree to that, then we'll do this without you.

That's not a threat, but it's the way it has to be. Please join us, and help us help you."

"I'll let my superiors know," he replied softly. "Head for the garage, and I'll meet you there in about five. We'll take a law enforcement van."

"I would prefer to remain low-profile. We can take our hover-van. It's leased for the duration of our stay."

"You mean the one where your driver was puking and has probably already quit?"

"I'll drive," Red offered.

"I'll have the uniformed driver meet us at your van if it's still there."

"And this is why we need him with us," Rivka explained. The empty van was where they'd left it, the blood dried to a dark brown on the floor. The driver was nowhere in sight.

"I could drive," Red said.

"Then you can't use your railgun, and we know how much you love Blazer." Rivka tapped her foot impatiently.

Five minutes became ten.

"You're driving, Red. Ankh, sit behind Red on the floor and call out the directions to keep us going the right way," Rivka directed. Jay climbed into the far back, with Lindy beside her. Rivka took the middle seat, and Ankh crouched between the driver's seat and the first row back. Rivka removed her jacket, tore off her stained shirt, and threw it on the floor, then put her jacket back on. "Okay, let's go."

Supra ran at them, yelling for them to wait.

"I'm sorry. Guvna had a lot of questions. The driver is on his way." Harpeth pointed to an approaching man.

Red threw open the driver's door and stepped out. He walked around the van to get into the first row, but Ankh was in the way.

The Crenellian pointed to the next row back.

"Ain't gonna happen," Red replied. He reached in and lifted Ankh out, standing him on the ground.

Ankh stared at the bodyguard. "I need to be able to see and react," Red clarified.

"Just sit in his lap," Rivka told them.

"No!" they declared in unison.

"Red, goddammit, make room." Rivka was starting to steam.

Red wedged himself against the side of the seat. He reached out and pulled Ankh in next to him. Ankh didn't take up much room, so Red relaxed and settled in.

"I'll sit up front." The supra started to get in as the driver fired up the engine.

"Sit back here with me so we can talk. I'd like to hear more about Collum Gate. This looks like an incredible place." Rivka smiled and patted the seat next to her.

"Where to?" the driver asked. Ankh gave him the address.

"Tell me about Collum Gate," Rivka requested when the hover-van had lifted into the air and started maneuvering toward the street.

"Collum Gate was established nearly two hundred years ago by a spacefaring race called the Sc'allid..." Rivka watched him and nodded every once in a while, but she was engaged in the conversation on the tactical communication system within their heads.

Did you see that he's not armed? I'm not taking responsibility for him, Red said.

Fine, I'll watch out for him, Lindy replied.

Bullshit! We watch the Magistrate first and the rest of the crew second. He's number eleven on our top ten list.

I'm not armed, Ankh said.

Neither is Jay, Rivka jumped into the conversation.

Are you sure about that? Lindy asked.

I didn't want to, but she made me. It's in the back of my pants, Jay interjected reluctantly.

What? Rivka tried to keep her exterior neutral while she found out who was packing what heat.

You *are,* Red emphasized to the Magistrate.

Of course, Rivka replied. *But I'm me, and you have neutron pulse envy. If I wasn't here, you'd be carrying it.*

Damn straight. Blazer and Dealy, bringing evil to its knees.

His is Blazer, but yours is Dealy? Jay remarked.

Mine is Mabel, Lindy admitted.

"Rivka?" the supra said more loudly to get her attention.

"I'm sorry," Rivka stuttered. "I was thinking about the case. I get lost that way. Federation Law is streamlined, but it's still plenty complex. I am concerned about the breadcrumbs."

"Breadcrumbs? I don't understand."

"It's from an old human children's story. It's pretty horrific if you think about it, but scaring our children seems to never go out of style. The children left breadcrumbs so they could find their way out from the evil witch's lair, or something like that. We follow the clues like breadcrumbs. We only need one to get us started."

"I see," Supra Harpeth said, pursing his lips and looking out the window. "We're almost there. Pull past and let us off around the corner."

Red lifted Ankh over his lap as the two changed seats.

"Why do humans have to be so big?" Ankh asked the window.

Red shrugged and clutched his railgun to his chest. He watched through the front window before leaning down to see to the rooftops of the buildings to their left. The nondescript but stylized building to their right housed the servers they were after. Somewhere deep within, the signals were intercepted and then sent to recipients who could be anywhere in the galaxy.

Ankh shared none of his concerns about the myriad of tendrils that might lead from the communications node. He and Erasmus had no doubts that they'd figure it out. All they needed was time. "I need time with the computers," Ankh found himself saying out loud.

"We'll give you as much as you need," Rivka assured the Crenellian.

The architecture of Collum Gate was nonlinear, consisting of curves and rounded corners. The humans were shocked at the imbalance within single structures. Windows would be on different levels and were different sizes. Taking in a block as a whole, balance would be restored. Comparably-sized buildings swept upward as mirrors of their counterparts, individually discordant, but taken together, they comprised a symphony.

Rivka admired what she saw. When they turned the

corner, she was introduced to yet another block of flowing buildings. The hover-van jerked to the right and slowed. When it stopped, Red opened the door and jumped out, hurrying to the corner where they'd just turned. He assessed the area. No open windows opposite. No observers on any rooftops that would hold them. Many flowed to a point, and wouldn't support someone outside. Red appreciated that aspect of the architecture.

The others disembarked, and Lindy held them back. Red gave the thumbs-up and headed down the street, startling a woman with two small children. She turned and ran the other way. Red led the group to the target building's entrance.

"Keep Ankh out of sight," Red called over his shoulder before he went inside. Rivka stayed on one side of the Crenellian with Supra Harpeth on the other, and Jay followed. Lindy stayed between the group and the roadway where hover-vehicles of various types flew past.

The road surface was a fine carpet of greenery, grass that helped fuel the planet's oxygen supply. No wheeled vehicles remained on Collum Gate since the planet's leadership strived to present a modern appearance while retaining the old world charm.

They used that to welcome alien races to incorporate a part of their world into the culture of Collum Gate.

Or used to.

Now people ran in fear.

Red walked into the lobby of an apartment building. There were no signs, and stairs to the left led both upward and downward. In the middle, an open elevator door beckoned.

"Which way, Ankh?" Red asked as he scanned the small area, his railgun pointing where his eyes looked.

"Down," the Crenellian answered.

"Looks like a tight squeeze. Don't bunch up." A double-wide stairway went up, but a narrow set of stairs led downward.

"At least they're well-lit," Rivka suggested after they had descended through the first two turnbacks. "How deep does this go?"

The lights went out.

CHAPTER TEN

Rivka instantly pulled Ankh behind her. She stared into the darkness below. A hint of light remained. Her enhanced and oversized eyes pulled in all there was until Red's outline appeared. She focused on him and saw more detail as her eyes further adjusted, including a shadow. To the big man's right, squeezing into the corner, unnoticed, with a long blade in hand.

Red, armed person at your three o'clock low, Rivka said over the comm.

With a vicious swing, he brought his railgun through the space. It connected with a heavy thud, and whoever was trying to ambush the group was thrown into the wall. The shadow crumpled to the landing without a sound.

Rivka hurried ahead. "Coming down behind you, Red." When she reached him, she warned him again. "I'm here, reaching around you to look below."

She leaned past him, making contact to let him know exactly where she was. He aimed his railgun into the darkness.

"I have a flashlight," he whispered.

"Not yet. Have it ready." She pulled his barrel lower. "I'm going to use Dealy. We can't destroy any more servers like we did with Nefas, but if this doesn't stop them, I'll need you to light them up."

She removed her neutron pulse weapon and aimed down the stairs to where three cloaked and hooded forms continued to climb slowly and silently upward. She dialed her weapon to nine and aimed at the shadowy figures.

"You can stop right there unless you want to die," Rivka warned. The three hesitated for only for a moment before continuing toward her.

Rivka fired. From below came grunts and screams from the wounded, their innards reduced to slush. They turned to run, but died before descending a single step and tumbled down the stairs.

"Lights," Rivka said evenly. Red clicked on his flashlight. Behind them, Lindy shone hers into the corner of the landing.

"What if those people didn't do anything wrong?" the supra asked, his eyes glistening under the flashlights' beams. He bent down to check the body. "I'm going to have to report this."

"I don't give a fuck what you do," Rivka growled. "We're in the presence of something dark. I can feel it."

It was like a raincloud that hung just over one's head, threatening to spill sheets of water on the masses below, merciless in its torrent.

Rivka joined Harpeth in looking at the corpse. She pulled the dark cloak away to reveal a young woman, willowy thin, in a skin-tight bodysuit. A sheath hung on her hip. Beside it, a curved thirty-centimeter blade had fallen from her hand.

"Is this your standard accouterment for a casual day out?" Rivka asked the supra. He gazed at it open-mouthed. Rivka picked the weapon up and passed it back to Jay.

"So young." He put his fingers over her eyes and brushed downward as if he needed to confirm that they were closed. He clenched his teeth. This was his town, and these were his people. Something was going on, and he didn't know what. He was more embarrassed than anything. He wanted to be upset by how quickly the Magistrate killed people, but ambassadors were dying, and this was a step toward finding those responsible. He wrestled with justifying the Magistrate's methods. He made his decision. "I can't be a part of this."

"Then go outside and wait for me." Rivka put a hand on his shoulder and continued in a hushed tone, "It's okay if this isn't for you. Magistrates have to deal with the very worst the universe has to offer. When violence is called for, we have no choice but to outdo the criminals. As they say, don't bring a knife to a gunfight."

She dismissed him with a wave of her hand. The supra slowly made his way between those standing on the stairs. Ankh moved to the landing and checked the sprawled body. He removed a pair of goggles from her head, loosened the band, and strapped them on.

"Turn off the flashlights, please," he requested, and they did as he asked. Rivka kept her focus down the stairs, watching the landing below where the jumbled bodies lay.

"Night-vision goggles, thin and high resolution. I shall keep these. You can turn the lights back on." Ankh pushed the goggles to his forehead and waited while Red slowly moved downward. He dipped around the landing and pulled back in case anyone was waiting. He'd seen nothing but a closed door at the bottom of the next flight of stairs. He removed a pair of goggles from one of the bodies and put them on.

Lindy, take one of these sets of goggles and give the other to Jay, Red told them. He passed the two sets to Rivka, who handed them back to Jay and Lindy. They extinguished both flashlights and put them on.

"Sweet," Red whispered.

He continued down the stairs, with Rivka close behind and Ankh casually strolling after them. Jay enjoyed the goggles, waving the knife to see it in the light-green glow by which she was seeing in the dark. Lindy brought up the rear, her railgun pointed at the wall. She turned her head in all directions, enjoying the ability to see without having to carry a flashlight.

Do you hear anything? Rivka asked.

A mechanical hum. Nothing that sounds like people. Red kept his observations clear and concise.

When he reached the door, he stopped.

Anything I should know before going in, Ankh? Keep in mind that I have a railgun, Red requested.

Don't shoot any of the equipment. It's best if you don't shoot anything in that room, Ankh replied.

I think we've already dealt with the guards. The people in that room shouldn't be armed, should they? Lindy ventured.

Magistrate, can I have Dealy?

You can borrow Reaper, Rivka replied. Red shrugged one shoulder before he reached an empty hand back. Rivka slapped the neutron pulse weapon into it. *We could use a couple more of those if you have any lying around.*

There is only one of those, and I'm appalled at how cavalierly you treat it! Ankh shot back.

It's called field testing, and we're doing it up right. You'll have our report soon.

Really? Ankh wondered.

No.

Rivka didn't need to turn around to see his goggled eyes staring at her. Jay moved in front of the Crenellian, brandishing her blade as she put herself between the door and him.

Lindy, protect Ankh no matter what happens, Rivka ordered.

What's going to happen? she asked.

On three, Red interrupted, and when he'd counted down, he rammed into the door. It was locked and didn't budge. The only thing he'd accomplished was announcing their arrival. He took two steps back and powered into the door, but it remained steadfast in denying entry. Red saw where the bolts were in place.

"Fire in the hole!" he yelled and took aim.

"Don't..." Ankh started to say, his voice disappeared into the skull-bouncing thunder from the hypervelocity darts shredding the locks. Red jammed through, dropping the railgun to hang from its sling as he took aim with the neutron pulse weapon.

Movement drew his eye, nothing more than a shadow darting behind a stack of electronics. The room was filled with equipment bathed in muted light, colored indicators flashing in syncopation.

Sprawling, yet haphazard, the room had a purpose. It was cold. Much better for the equipment than heat. Heavy power cables were strung through the open overhead. Red rushed to the first bank of computers and leaned around, counting on the goggles to see into the dark corners.

"Coming around the end!" Red called.

Rivka had followed Red in, suddenly alarmed at being unarmed.

A figure appeared and darted toward the door. She stuck out her leg, sending the individual tripping and face first into the floor at Jay's feet. She touched her blade against the side of the person's neck.

"How many more are in here?" Rivka demanded, rushing over to grab the person's arm. A woman. Thin and pale. The woman's mind ran under the dark cloud of fear.

None.

She was telling the truth. Rivka added in a gentle voice, "Let her up."

Jay kept her blade aimed at the woman with the adult face but a youth's body.

"That's all there were in here. We're clear," Rivka told Red. He nodded and signaled for everyone to stay where they were as he quickly explored the rest of the room. Two minutes later the lights came on in the room and stairway. The goggles adjusted instantly, protecting the wearers from getting blinded.

Red removed his and carefully put them into a pocket. Ankh pulled his up, letting them rest on his oversized forehead. Jay and Lindy followed Ankh's lead.

"It's your show. We're looking for the next breadcrumb," Rivka said.

"Put one of the coins I gave you inside that server," Ankh directed, pointing.

"I don't have them," Rivka replied.

"Where are they?"

"On the ship," Rivka said softly.

"What good are they on the ship?" Ankh asked in his neutral voice. Rivka suspected he was annoyed.

Red held out a hand with one of Ankh's devices.

"Why do you have these?" Rivka wondered.

"I thought they might be useful," Red answered. "Just like grenades."

"You have grenades?" Supra Harpeth asked, appearing in the doorway. Lindy jumped, earning a harsh look from Red.

"Don't you?" Red shrugged one shoulder.

Ankh sat down while Rivka remedied her shortsightedness by emplacing the device Red had given her. The Crenellian disappeared into thought, and the group waited.

"What made you change your mind?" Rivka asked.

"My superiors registered my complaint with the Federation, earning themselves a call directly from Lance Reynolds. I wanted to express my heartfelt apology for not fully supporting your efforts to save me from my failure to resolve this case." The supra held his hands before him as if praying.

"You were told to apologize or be fired?"

"Something like that."

"If they ask, I'll tell them that your words brought tears to my eyes."

"Might be a little much," Harpeth replied, but nodded and smirked.

"I doubt they'll question my veracity." Rivka slapped him on the shoulder. Red watched, casually cradling Blazer. Rivka held out her hand. He slapped something into her palm. She held up his flashlight and thrust it at him.

"Mine." He swapped the neutron pulse weapon. The Magistrate happily shoved Reaper into her pocket. "Is this the infamous server farm?"

Ankh was in his own world, oblivious to what was going on around him. He wouldn't be answering any questions. But there was someone else who knew.

"We need you to tell us what you know," Rivka said to the woman. "Start with your name."

The woman didn't look belligerent, only terrified. Her jaw worked, but she couldn't form words.

"Jay, put that thing away and help her calm down."

She looked for a place to stash the blade, but couldn't find one. She finally gave it to Lindy for safekeeping. The bodyguard took it and returned to the landing on the stairs where she could watch for intruders. While there, she relieved the body of its sheath, clipping it onto her ballistic vest and stuffing the long blade into it.

Lindy relaxed and settled in, making sure that no one surprised the team as Harpeth had done when she had become too interested in the room below and not the security of those in her charge. She understood why Red was so hard on himself. A moment's loss of concentration could be the difference between life and death. Her lip curled at the thought.

Red had told her there was much to learn and that it required a different mindset, shutting out everything the

Magistrate was doing except how an enemy might take advantage. Much to learn indeed, but she had Mabel for comfort, and her big man to teach her.

"Bring the van out front," the supra said into his communication device.

Lindy led the way up the stairs, with Jay and Ankh behind, then Rivka, Harpeth cuffed to the prisoner, and Red.

It had been twenty minutes since they'd breached the server room. It took Ankh less than ten minutes to learn its secrets and give them two leads. The caretaker was in the wrong place at the wrong time. She hadn't spoken, which led the supra to commit to keeping at her until she told them who'd hired her.

"I don't understand the reason for the security. People wearing dark cloaks and carrying knives. What was that all about?"

"Gaining the tactical edge," Red offered. "With only one way in or out, they would die in place without getting the drop on any intruders. It was their one-time use plan. Don't forget that they had the high-res night vision goggles."

"But why? I can't believe the computers were important enough that five people were hired to protect them."

"They were," Ankh offered without further explanation.

Supra Harpeth stepped over the bodies. "When can we get our people in here?"

"As soon as we walk out the door, Supra," Rivka said,

"but keep this place locked down. We may need to return. No matter what, I don't want any outsiders in here messing with the equipment."

Ankh waved a dismissive hand. "There are tracking programs on all of it. The only way to remove them is to completely wipe the servers and start over. We're fine no matter what they do."

"You are amazing, Ankh. Thank you for joining the crew, and before you ask, the answer is yes. You can keep the goggles."

"I wasn't going to ask that," Ankh deadpanned.

Rivka turned back to Harpeth. "You'll probably need armed guards here, too. I suspect our perp won't appreciate our intrusion into his or her affairs. It also means we move fast. We follow every breadcrumb as soon as we find it, while the trail is hot. And you need to keep *her* in custody until we've found who we're looking for."

"Is that how you roll? Hit the ground running and only speed up from there?"

"I'd like to say that I adjudicate cases at a measured pace, but that would be misleading. The pace is frenetic. Criminals don't need to enjoy freedom one second longer than necessary. It pains me that they breathe the same air as good people."

"Our legal system doesn't enjoy the same level of passion that you have, but we don't have to carry the burdens of an entire galaxy."

Rivka was frowning when they reached the small entry area.

Harpeth motioned for his people to get to work. "Four bodies on the stairs and an equipment room with a busted door. Secure the room and recover the bodies. Keep the room under armed guard until I cancel the order."

The stiga—the investigator—saluted and waved two petros, uniformed patrol officers, to him to take a post at the top of the stairs. Four more petros and two specialists headed down to clean up the mess.

"It must be nice to just walk away from something like that. I'll be quagmired in the paperwork for weeks."

Rivka stopped him. "Killing people is never nice. Chasing people who kill people isn't nice. You know what's nice? Sitting around doing the paperwork, and bitching about the people who do the hard work. If you keep whining, I'll send you packing. Is that clear?"

Supra Harpeth was all too aware of his attitude. He grimaced and slowly shook his head. "You're right. I don't deserve the honor of working with the first Magistrate to visit our planet."

"Shut up and get in the van," Rivka told him. Red was first into the open and waited to the side while the others hurried from the building and into the waiting vehicle.

Lindy closed the door behind her.

"Where to, Ankh?"

"The Collum Daily building," the Crenellian replied.

"The news outlet?" Harpeth asked.

"The news outlet."

CHAPTER ELEVEN

"The police can't raid the news," Harpeth said.

"The police won't be," Rivka replied before leaning over the seat to look at the back of the Crenellian's head. "What are we looking for, Ankh?"

"We are looking for a switch."

Red shrugged. Harpeth didn't know. Jay and Lindy had no idea. Lindy was admiring the sheath and the long knife.

"You'll have to clue in us lesser mortals, Ankh. I don't know what you mean by a switch. Is that another computer?"

Ankh was wedged between Red and the window. He wasn't able to face Rivka, so he talked to the back of the driver's seat. "A switch is a switch. It takes a signal from the outside and routes in one of multiple directions. I believe there is one that is manually activated. Someone at the news station is sending decoded signals to third parties."

"Decoded? That's what the equipment in the basement did." Rivka rubbed her chin as she tried to form the web in her mind of where the signals were being routed and rerouted.

"Yes. Our original signal was diverted through those servers, where it was decrypted and retransmitted directly to the Collum Daily's offices. Most of the information stays there. Supra, have you ever wondered why the news outlet seemed to have the latest on everything? They are stealing classified information. And, by narrowing who publishes the scoops, we need to talk with Nat Ferider. She is the recipient of the information."

The supra's mouth fell open, and he gawked. "That's not possible. She's a respected journalist and treats people decently, even in articles that expose tough information. She wouldn't be a criminal."

"We don't have to judge until we get more information. I'll talk to her myself and get to the bottom of it in short order. What did you say, Ankh? There's a manual switch?"

"Yes." The Crenellian didn't waste any words.

With Supra Harpeth leading the way, the group headed for the senior editor's office.

"Hang on a second." Rivka removed her datapad and pulled up a picture of the person she was there to find. She showed it to Lindy. "Why don't you stay here? If she shows up, could you hang onto her for us?"

"Bodyguard," Red warned.

"She's been promoted," Rivka replied. "She's now a direct action intervention and security services specialist."

"You're making that up," Red said, shaking his head.

"Damn straight." Rivka turned back to Lindy. "Don't let her get past you. We don't have time to waste looking for someone who doesn't want to be found. We already have at least one of those. I don't want any more."

"Will do. I'll be outside." Lindy tipped her chin to Red, and he smiled back.

"I suppose you're going to make an impassioned plea to unload the mech," Rivka said as Red watched Lindy walk away. Jay punched him in the arm.

"What was that for?"

"You were staring at her butt."

"And?" Red scanned the surrounding area. Nothing had changed in the ten seconds since he'd last evaluated it for threats. He smiled, the image of Lindy still in his mind. "We need to move. Standing around always makes me nervous."

"Stand now, run later! That's our mantra," Rivka suggested, ushering Harpeth to the front.

"I don't understand, but that's okay. You off-worlders have your own ways, which we welcome even if we don't understand them."

The entire first floor of the Collum Daily building was a cubicle farm. As the sole source for news on the planet, they sported a large staff that was perpetually busy. Based on the government's guidance, the *Daily* had restricted their speculative articles about the murders so they didn't create a panic. The information was already being circulated in the diplomatic channels. There was less anxiety within the populace than the Collum Gate leadership expected to see.

It was common to hear, "They're just aliens."

Rivka was aware that the locals were trending toward

supporting the killer. It didn't change her job, but it did affect how she looked at the locals. Even Harpeth had tried to distance himself from the investigation, which had been alarmingly lean on evidence and facts.

The Magistrate was starting to wonder if it was a worldwide conspiracy. Her expression told everyone that her thoughts were troubled.

They walked up a wide and ornate staircase to the level where the senior editor's office was located. He chose not to be on the top floor so he could be in the middle of the action and stay in touch with the reporters.

There was no cordon they had to pass, no security, only a couple of junior editors who filtered the volume before it reached the boss.

"We're here to see the senior editor," Harpeth told the person closest to the door. The woman didn't even look up as she pointed over her shoulder with her thumb. She stopped and looked up when Red towered over her desk.

"What are you?" she blurted, pushing her chair away from the man mountain.

"Personal security for the Magistrate," Red replied without looking at her. "What are you?"

He didn't *have* to snark back, but the locals were putting him in a foul mood.

"I'm an editor with the *Collum Daily*. Maybe you've heard of it?"

"The fact that I'm standing here suggests I have. Are all the *Daily*'s employees arrogant assholes like you?"

She harrumphed her outrage. Rivka made eye contact with Red before turning toward the senior editor's door. She tried not to laugh at her bodyguard's retort, but her patience was wearing thin, too. They'd been on the planet for mere hours and had already been attacked.

Twice. She was wearing her jacket without a shirt, which was liberating but less than professional. Lindy was wearing her bloodstained clothes, which was less than optimal.

Harpeth knocked twice and opened the door. Inside was a harried-looking man sitting in the middle of a holo-projector. Screens twisted and danced around him as he viewed videos, read headlines, and looked through random paragraphs of Collum script.

"We'll come back later if you're busy," Supra Harpeth offered.

"We'll talk now," Rivka corrected. "Ankh, can you shut that off, please?"

The Crenellian strolled to the console, reached through the holographic image, and tapped a button. The holo-screens receded into the console.

"Excuse me!" the man declared loudly, looking angrily at the supra.

Rivka smiled and offered her hand. "I'm Magistrate Rivka from the Federation here to investigate the ambassadors' murders." She left it open to see if the senior editor would give something away. She thrust her hand closer, and he finally took it.

His disdain for the Federation jumped to the front of his mind. When he looked at Ankh, he recalled a short piece related to the attempt on the Crenellian's life—an article written by the journalist they were looking for.

Now was the perfect time. She held his hand as she

asked her first question. "What do you know about Nat Ferider and her relationship with the serial killer?"

Doubt filled his mind. He never questioned his journalists and their sources, but hers had been unparalleled in its accuracy and the speed with which she'd produced the stories. He believed Ferider was in on it. *Despair!* His soul cried out in anguish. He pulled his hand free and collapsed into his chair, burying his face in his hands.

"I don't know anything about that. She's a good journalist. One of our best," he finally said.

"We need to talk to her," Rivka stated flatly.

"Up one level, corner office," he mumbled through his fingers.

Rivka pointed at the door. When they went outside, they found the junior editor on her personal communication device. Red pulled it from her hand, clicked it off, and dropped it in the trash can before continuing toward the stairs.

"Gossip is such an ugly thing," Jay told her. Jay swished her platinum blue hair in an arc past the woman's face as they walked away.

What kind of thugs have we become? Rivka asked over their internal comm system. *Red, don't do that kind of shit.*

It won't happen again, Magistrate. She pissed me off, but that's no excuse. She was no threat to you, so I shouldn't have given her a millisecond of my time.

Thanks, Red. That's good focus. I don't know what it is, but something's not right here. These people are putting me on edge, too.

It's the diplomatic influence, Ankh suggested.

I don't understand, Rivka replied.

I know this one! Jay exclaimed. *In diplomatic circles, there is much said that isn't true. Perception is the only reality, so they maintain false fronts. The serial killer—is that what we're calling him now?—has destroyed the facade. Without that, the real world becomes an ugly place.*

Is that what you saw from your parents? Rivka asked. They reached the steps and started to climb.

All the time and way too much. They were two very different people, depending on which side of the door they were standing on.

We need to find this person and put them out of our misery so we can get off this planet.

I'm wondering when the island paradise mission will come, Red remarked.

The third floor was busier than the first two. A person brushed by and rushed down the stairs, then a second person. A third one had her face buried in a folder, mumbling as she walked by. Rivka turned after she'd gone by to watch her.

"Nat?" she called. The woman threw the folder as she leapt down the next three steps and started to run. Jay froze, putting a protective arm around Ankh. Rivka shrugged and started walking back down the stairs. Red took the flight of stairs in two jumps, getting into a position where he could see the fleeing suspect. The supra followed.

Our suspect is running down the stairs and headed toward you, Red passed to Lindy over their internal comm channel. He slowed to a walk as he watched the woman race between the cubicles. Just before she reached the door, Lindy stepped through. She hit Nat Ferider in the chest with an arm bar. The journalist's feet came out from under her as she upended, spun in the air, and slammed face-first into the floor.

Lindy picked the gasping woman up with one hand and started dragging her toward the stairs.

Rivka waved them to where she waited on the landing. Red dominated the top of the stairs, holding his railgun across his chest. He was in full combat gear, including his combat helmet.

All of the employees saw the exchange. It was hard to miss the Daily's number one journalist running from a bunch of newcomers, only to be intercepted and body-slammed. Recording devices peeked above cubicle walls to capture the video.

"Ankh, I don't want any of that video or an article about this to hit the street for twenty-four hours. If you would be so kind..." Rivka requested.

The Crenellian's eyes unfocused as he communed with his AI. His night-vision goggles were prominently displayed on his forehead. He didn't care what he looked like.

And neither did Rivka, when she thought about it. He did his job well.

I've put a scrubbing program in place to lock out the videos. One was already uploaded but has been quarantined. We've discovered thirty-one recordings on the floor below. Erasmus has locked them within their devices, and further recording will not be possible within this building for the next twenty-four hours. Does this mean that the investigation will be complete by then?

"It will have to be. The perp has to know we're on his or her tail. Will they be brazen and hide in plain sight? We'll see what we can learn when we find this switch and ask a few questions of our dashing new friend," Rivka replied.

Lindy shoved the woman up the stairs to land at Red's feet. "Get up and come with us."

"Who…who are you?" Nat stammered.

"You didn't think to ask that before you started running? What are you afraid of?" Rivka asked as she gripped the woman's arm and helped her up.

Fear of being found out. Fear of losing her stature. Fear of the faceless and nameless entity she funneled information to. Fear that she was finished.

Rivka almost felt sorry for her. Almost.

"You wanted to be the number-one journalist on the planet, so you crawled into bed with evil. How did you expect that to turn out?" Rivka jerked the woman to get her attention. "Never mind. Just show us the switch, that thing you flipped to send supposedly secure information to the murderer. You *do* know what that makes you, don't you?"

Rivka's face was inches from the journalist's.

The woman started sobbing uncontrollably. Rivka grabbed her by the ears and growled into her face. "Show us, or I swear I will punch my hand into your chest and rip out your beating heart! Where's the switch?"

It flashed into her mind—one simple toggle under her desk with a lead going into the drawer. The drawer was coded, but Rivka had seen the numbers.

"Bring her," the Magistrate ordered. Lindy twisted the woman's arm behind her back and pushed. Supra Harpeth finally stepped up, showing a pair of stylish handcuffs. He secured her arms behind and guided her up the stairs.

Lindy stayed far enough behind to prevent any runs for freedom. Red took his usual position and headed back up the stairs. He started to perspire. The heavier gravity was weighing them all down and probably contributed to their short tempers.

Jay was holding Ankh's hand as if she were leading a child. Her right hand remained free and on the hilt of the long knife at her side. A lump in the small of her back showed where she kept the pistol. Rivka could understand why someone would be intimidated by the Magistrate's team. That couldn't be helped, because they *needed* to be intimidating. They had to deal with the worst the galaxy had to offer.

Nefas hadn't been intimidated. He hadn't cared. The worst criminals didn't since they thought they were the biggest and the baddest.

What will this switch tell you? Rivka asked.

Where the signal goes next. The breadcrumbs.

Follow the breadcrumbs, Rivka reiterated. *Thanks, Ankh.*

When the group reached the journalist's office, the door was locked. Red didn't bother asking for the key. He hip-checked it, splitting the doorframe. The door swung inward, showing a desk with screens, bookshelves, and meager decorations. It was a working journalist's office.

Rivka walked around the desk and kneeled to look underneath.

"Here," she told Ankh. He bent down to look at it.

"We need to get in there." Ankh pointed at the lower desk drawer. "Unless you have one of the coins I gave you."

Rivka glared at Ankh briefly. They'd already covered that ground.

She punched in the code, and the drawer opened. "It's all yours."

He leaned down to study the electronics within.

"How'd you do that?" Nat Ferider asked, her eyes puffy and red from crying.

"Tell us more about your contact," Rivka stated, wrapping her fingers around the journalist's wrist.

"You're hurting me," Nat complained.

"You're an accessory to a serial killer. In the Federation, that's a capital crime. As a Magistrate, I can pass judgment right fucking now. Do you understand?"

"But I didn't *do* anything!" she groaned, and the tears started to flow afresh.

"The information you received about the arriving Crenellian ambassador? That was him." Rivka pointed to Ankh, two arms deep into the drawer. "I got shot for it. If I wasn't special, I'd be dead. What do you want from me, forgiveness?"

"Yes," she muttered. Harpeth held her tightly to keep her from falling. "I'm innocent."

"Now you're a liar in addition to an accessory to multiple murders and an attempted murder." Rivka let go of her arm. She wasn't getting anything new. The woman didn't know who she was transmitting the information to. She suspected, but remained willfully ignorant. "You know the best thing about being me?" Rivka waited. "I don't care about your plea. I know what's in your mind. I've seen what you've done through your own eyes. You are as guilty as sin. You will be banished from this job since you can't be trusted to report the news, having demonstrated a willingness to create the news instead.

And because you have caused so many people physical pain, uncuff her."

Supra was confused but did as the Magistrate ordered.

"Now give me your shirt." Rivka snapped her fingers. "I said, give me your shirt. Because of you, my last one was ruined. *Give me your shirt.*"

The woman did as ordered, standing there in just her bra, trying to cover herself with her hands.

"Give me your hand." Rivka held hers out, rock-steady. Nat Ferider put her hands behind her back and shook her head. "I said, *give me your hand!*"

Rivka jabbed her in the stomach, and she instinctively brought her hands to the front. Rivka caught one and rammed it into the side of the desk, breaking three of the woman's fingers. She screamed and howled.

"Get out," Rivka growled and pointed at the door.

Nat looked like she wanted to say something but decided against it, cradling her injured digits over her fancy teal bra as she staggered from the office.

"Is that how you do things?" Supra Harpeth asked.

"She'll never forget the consequences of her crime. I'll file the report with your department, so you have it in case she runs afoul of the law again. I don't think you'll have any more problems with her, and isn't that what punishment is supposed to be about?"

"But you broke her fingers." Harpeth pointed to the spot on the desk, reliving the meting out of Justice.

"Yes, because her fingers threw the switch that sent intelligence to the killer. That intelligence was used to kill people. I could have executed her. Is that what you'd prefer?"

"Of course not. That's barbaric, just like physical punishment!" He stood as tall as he was able and looked down at her. Red bumped into him from behind.

"You'll not want to threaten the Magistrate," he said in a low and dangerous voice.

"Or what?"

Rivka held her hand up to stop Red before he pummeled the supra.

"You're off the case," Rivka said. She removed her data-pad. "Chaz, log an order with Collum Gate that Nat Ferider is a convicted felon and that she is prohibited from holding a public interest position. Also, report to law enforcement that Supra Harpeth has been removed from this case by my order. Thanks, Chaz. Now *you*, get out." She pointed at the door. He had to work his way around Red, who filled the empty space. Lindy locked eyes and glared at him.

CHAPTER TWELVE

Once the door was shut, Rivka took off her jacket and put the shirt on. She tossed the jacket over her shoulder, holding it casually with one hand.

"Now that we've alienated all the locals, what's our next stop?" Rivka asked.

Ankh stood up, holding the device, wires dangling from it.

"Erasmus has found a number of addresses that we need to visit."

"How many?" Rivka groaned.

"Only twelve."

"And I just fired the guy who could help us. I wonder if he'll leave the driver."

"We should probably go," Red suggested.

"Ankh?"

"Yes. We can go. I've shared the locations on your data-pad. You'll be able to see them on a map. We've calculated an optimal route to visit them as quickly as possible, although it would have been optimal to hit all twelve at once, just in case the killer is monitoring them."

Red opened the door and headed out.

"We don't have that option—unless we do. Lindy, can you run down Harpeth and tell him to wait? I want to talk to him."

"On my way, Magistrate." Lindy squeezed Red's butt before she accelerated across the floor and disappeared down the stairs.

When the Magistrate reached the first landing, she found Lindy and Harpeth.

"You didn't make it very far," Rivka quipped.

"I want you to reconsider," the supra said with his head bowed.

"Done!" Rivka declared happily. She checked the area to make sure no one was listening. "I need you to coordinate a simultaneous raid on twelve different properties. And we need to hit them only as soon as humanly possible. I have the coordinates."

She showed him the map on her datapad.

"Personal residences in different economic zones throughout the city. This is interesting. Each of them borders an alien district."

Jay had Ankh pulled tightly to her side, her arm wrapped protectively around him.

"You have separate housing areas for aliens, even if they don't need special accommodation?" Rivka asked.

"It's not like you're trying to make it sound," Harpeth replied, holding his hands up defensively. "They're just different areas, same everything else."

"I've been told that this planet is a peaceful place,

unused to violence. Now we have a shooting war because there are sides. The haves and have-nots. The tall versus the short. The wide versus the thin. The off-worlders and the Collum Gaters. I don't wish anyone harm, but it looks like separate but equal hasn't worked out."

"You can't judge us on the actions of one person!"

"Our thoughts become our attitudes become our words become our actions." Rivka held his gaze. "The killer may be acting alone, but there is a disgusting amount of sympathy for what this individual is doing. Like that woman with a few broken fingers who helped create the conditions for murdering aliens."

Rivka stopped. The journalist's office jumped into her mind. It had been low tech, except for what was hidden in the drawer.

"Ankh, who programmed the servers to decrypt diplomatic communications? It sure as hell wasn't Miss Prissy Pants."

"The signature within the code was H4rea78L. The code was sophisticated, on par with what we saw from the Mandolin Partnership. I don't think it was her. It may not have been the shooter, but someone the killer hired."

"What are we going to find at these twelve houses?" Harpeth asked. Ankh looked up at the supra but didn't answer.

"What do we need to tell the officers to look for?" Rivka clarified.

"The killer, of course. All of these homes are supposed to be vacant, but they all have significant energy signatures. They are occupied, and they were the places that received the signal when the switch was flipped. I put a tracking code in each of those places should they move the receiving equipment."

"You flipped the switch?"

"Once Erasmus had control over the system, yes. We reduced the number of variables and planted a false message."

"We just foiled an attack. Would they raise their heads again so soon?" Rivka wondered. She didn't think so.

"I planted the message that the key ambassadors would be meeting at the Forum tonight."

"But they *are* meeting tonight!" Harpeth blurted.

"There was nothing on the schedule and nothing in any of the servers that suggested this meeting. It was planted information."

"Yes, but they didn't tell anyone about it! I knew, but they asked that we not provide security. I changed who would patrol the area, but that's it. No one else knows besides the guvna."

Ankh's nostrils flared while his facial expression remained neutral. "We better find the killer before tonight," he said blandly.

Rivka breathed heavily, almost snorting like a bull ready to charge. It had been ninety minutes, but finally, the law enforcement was in place to conduct the simultaneous raids. Harpeth held his communicator up and tipped his chin toward Rivka.

"Don't wait on me. Light this candle, and let's go kick some ass."

"*Go! Go! Go!*" Supra Harpeth ordered.

"If all twelve places are occupied, how will we know which one is the killer?"

"All you have to do is detain the squatters. I'll do the rest. We'll get to the bottom of it."

The communicator crackled. The first takedown was over. One man in custody.

"Driver," Harpeth called, "take us to Nebula Court."

The hover-van lifted into the air and accelerated away. It whipped silently through the city, stopping first at the intersection since it didn't have emergency lights.

"Ankh?" Rivka asked.

"Green lights from here to there, Magistrate," Ankh said softly.

Instantly the light changed. The van careened through traffic, maintaining speed until the final turn onto the target road. Two law enforcement vehicles were parked out front, lights flashing. A squat and heavy man was cuffed and seated on the front step.

Red jumped out and held his hand back to keep anyone else from getting out until he'd visually scoured the area. He waved them out and stepped aside. His railgun was raised and tracing a figure eight through the air. Lindy climbed out last and added her railgun to his, covering an opposite sector, finger on the safety, ready to flip it off if she needed to engage.

Rivka marched straight to the man in handcuffs.

His lip twitched when he saw her approach, but he made no move to stand or speak.

She took a seat next to him and put her hand on his

shoulder before asking pleasantly, "What are you doing here?"

Watching the alien sector. Fury!

"Who do you report to?"

"What?" the man retorted.

Lost his job to alien technology that replaced the workers. Then lost his home. He was alone.

Rivka stood. "Let him go," she told the officers before turning back to him. "That alien technology you are so angry about is made by humans, just not here."

"How did you know?" he asked, standing and lifting his hands so he could be freed.

"I'm the Magistrate. It's my job to know things. Don't be angry at aliens. They had nothing to do with you losing your job. That was your people right here on Collum Gate. When one door closes..."

"I know, I know. A new one opens. Isn't that what you were going to say?"

"Something like that. Being angry? That isn't going to get you to a good place. Get yourself straight and get back to work. You'll feel better for it."

"But where? There aren't any jobs."

"I hear there's an opening at the *Collum Daily*. I'm sorry, that's not fair. Ankh?"

The Crenellian looked up at her. "Yes?"

"Job openings that he might be qualified for?"

"This is how you wish to employ an R2D2 researcher?" Ankh asked evenly.

"At this moment in time, that answer is yes."

Ankh turned to the man. "There is a new construction project opening not far from here. They are conducting interviews tomorrow. The response to their ad has been lackluster because the manual labor pool is limited. They've raised their starting rates to be more competitive."

"But I'm not the manual labor sort," the man complained.

Rivka twirled her finger in the air and pointed to the van. "Next!" she ordered.

Harpeth checked his device. "Suspect in custody at Beau Nair Place."

Lindy snorted, and Red smirked. Jay made no comment. "Next stop, Beau Nair," Rivka said slowly.

The hover-van headed out. Once again, they had green lights the whole way. The driver smiled as he drove the leased van at breakneck speeds, something he would have never been able to do, even with lights flashing and in pursuit.

Five suspects later, they were no closer to finding a perp. Rivka sat with her head hanging down.

"We're down to a one in six chance," Jay suggested. "It's better than where we started."

"A d6 instead of a d12? I'll take those odds," Red replied.

"You don't play that game, do you?"

"Of course. Helps me stay on my toes, teaches me how to work in a team, problem-solving, and tactical and strategic thinking. It's the whole mental training package. The question should be, Magistrate, why don't *you* play?"

"Who do you play with?"

"Right now, the computer, but Lindy is almost ready to

give it a shot. We can play in the red room. Get the whole crew on board."

"I'm pretty sure 'almost ready' is a stretch," Lindy muttered.

"When are we going to visit the Crenellians?" Ankh asked, his voice small.

"As soon as we finish with these final six." Rivka put a comforting hand on his shoulder. He flinched but settled back. No emotions washed over Rivka. No images jumped into her mind. His was the difference between a mind wracked with emotion and a disciplined, controlled mind.

At the next stop, they found two suspects in custody. A man and a woman, both angry, snarling at their captors like wild dogs.

"Red, Lindy, I may need your assistance with this pair."

She reached toward them in the way that earned her the nickname "Zombie." They recoiled until Red and Lindy held them still. The pair snapped their teeth at the bodyguards. Red elbowed the man in the head. Lindy pulled back on the woman's hair until she grunted in pain.

"What are you doing here?" Rivka asked for the seventh time.

The man gritted his teeth and glared.

"He's the one. Take them both in," Rivka said in relief. In his mind, he'd seen her before—through the scope of his weapon, right before he pulled the trigger. "Where's the rifle?"

He tried to fight her the instant he realized that she was in his mind, but it was too late.

"Floorboards in the attic. Dig it out and bring it. Tear

the house apart looking for anything else. We have a knifing and a bombing to account for."

She was concerned that she hadn't seen those crimes in his mind. Maybe the woman.

Rivka grabbed her. "What was your role in the murders?"

"What murders?" the woman shot back. Confusion. She'd seen them on the news but knew nothing otherwise.

The man had concealed everything from her.

"She doesn't know anything, but bring her along anyway. Keep her apart from him. And I want to talk with those in the last five places. Bring them to the station."

The officers threw the two in separate vehicles and with lights flashing, they headed out.

"Easy as that?" Red asked as Rivka pointed toward the house. "These things are always so anti-climactic. We're running with our hair on fire, and then the perp's in custody. We wipe our hands of it and go on our merry way."

"I'm happy that we stopped the killer. That we did it quickly, in a relative sense, is an added bonus. We couldn't have done it without Ankh, our newest and most valuable member of the team."

"I couldn't agree more," Jay said, grimacing as she looked in the wardrobe at the smattering of off colors and discordant designs.

They opened drawers and lifted mattresses while they waited for the officer to retrieve the weapon.

"What's taking so long?" Rivka said and started up the ladder into the attic crawlspace. Red grabbed her.

"You get the feeling that something is wrong? Let me go first," he said.

Red raised his pistol and pulled his knife. With one in each hand, he carefully climbed the ladder. He poked his head through the opening and ducked back out.

"Officer's down," Red whispered. "Looks empty, but no one come up here until I give the all clear."

He lifted himself through the opening and into the attic, crouching low to move toward the downed petro. The man's skin had already turned purple. He'd only been dead for a few minutes.

Red examined what he could see before flipping the man over. A needle lashed out from beneath and scratched the back of Red's hand, burning like fire. Red rubbed it on his vest, clenching his teeth against the pain.

Rivka had climbed the ladder and was watching him.

"Don't touch the body. Poison trap." Red cradled his hand as his nanocytes fought against the invading toxin. He studied the flipped body. With his boot, he stomped the activation triggers and destroyed the traps arrayed around the weapon. He poked with the butt of his railgun to make sure there weren't additional traps before levering the rifle from its place. He held it up. "Got it."

"Anything else in there?"

Red scooped out a small bag. "Ammunition, and there's not much of it." Red stepped aside so Rivka could look in. The scratch on his hand was already closed. He wiggled his fingers. "Still tingling."

"If that had happened a few months ago, you would have been dead."

"Maybe. I'm quite the specimen if you haven't noticed."

"Really?" Lindy called from the opening where she stood on the ladder. She glanced toward the body. "Is he dead?"

"I'm afraid so," Rivka replied. She took hold of his ankles. "Grab his arms."

Red crouched to lift his end of the officer and crab-walked toward the opening. They sat the body upright, and Rivka let him fall over her shoulder before she descended the ladder. The Magistrate continued down the stairs and into the yard. Supra Harpeth groaned and hurried to help.

"There was a trap in the attic. Poison." Rivka felt bad for the officer and his family. The perp had been caught. There was no reason for anyone else to die. When she'd seen the malice in his mind alongside the image of the rifle, she hadn't seen the trap he'd set. To him, it was a trivial thing. To the officer on the ground, it had been life and death.

Evil saw the world differently. Psychopaths had no remorse. Ever. Rivka didn't look forward to further interrogations, but she needed to know.

Where was the bomb-making equipment?

CHAPTER THIRTEEN

Rivka's crew was subdued when they arrived at the law enforcement center. Harpeth hadn't made it yet since he'd taken the body to the morgue. He also committed to turning the rifle in for forensic examination.

The Magistrate wanted to send a message to the ambassadors, but in a couple of hours, they would be together to talk about the serial killer. In the meantime, Rivka intended to further interrogate the perp.

It appeared that the guvna had different plans. He intercepted Rivka and her crew. "I cannot thank you enough for your help in resolving this case," he said in a slimy politician's voice. He thrust out his hand, and when Rivka took it, he pumped hers over-enthusiastically.

Get off my planet! screamed in his mind. Rivka chuckled and pulled him close. "We're not leaving until I talk to him."

The guvna's smile faded slowly. "I'm sorry, but in this matter, we've reinstated an ancient law that allows capital punishment. In accordance with Federation Law, if we apply the Federation standard in the adjudication, we can reestablish jurisdiction as long as the accused is a Collum Gate citizen, which he is."

"You're refusing to let me see him?" Rivka said in a stone-cold tone. Red rolled his shoulders to make sure his railgun clanked against his gear.

"Refuse? That's a sensational word. We are freeing you to return to your duties. It's a big galaxy, and we're only one small planet. Our issue is between us and our people. We need to resolve it. I'm sure you understand."

"I do understand, Guvna. I understand that you want to take credit for the apprehension. I don't care about the credit, but I do care about the resolution. I don't think he worked alone, and I need to talk with him and get confirmation. That's what I want. You can grandstand all you want, but I have a case that isn't closed until I say it's closed."

"I'm afraid you have no case. It is back in our hands now. If all goes as we expect, he'll be executed by this evening."

"What?" Rivka was outraged. "Why in the hell would you rush that?"

"We have everything we need. Do you know that under our law, an execution is carried out using the convicted's own weapon?"

Rivka shook her head. She was trying to think through the law, but she was too angry to make sense of it. "We'll return to my ship, but this isn't over. Not by a long stretch."

The guvna held his hands out, palms out by way of an apology. Rivka stormed from the station to find the hover-van parked without a driver.

"Do you think they recalled their driver, now that they consider the case to be closed?"

"Undoubtedly," Jay said. "It's what my parents would do. Make the situation so uncomfortable that the person ended up doing what they wanted. Our presence here has been uncomfortable from the word go. Now that you've done their job for them, they're ratcheting up the pressure."

"You have wisdom beyond your years, Jayita. Thanks for joining the team."

"I'm not telling you anything you don't already know. I haven't contributed much on this one, but I will protect Ankh while the others protect you. You two are doing all the legal work. I guess you can refer to me as the hired muscle." To emphasize her point, Jay lifted her arms and flexed her biceps.

Red laughed out loud, recovered quickly, and went back to watching for threats.

"No driver. Looks like you're the wheelman, Red."

"Wheelman in a vehicle with no wheels. No one up front with me, please. Lindy by the side door. Everyone else, stay frosty. I don't trust anyone on this planet."

"You're not alone." Rivka joined Vered in an examination of the hover-van. A bomb would ruin their day. "Ankh, can you look under there and see if there's anything that's not supposed to be there?"

"Why me? Is it because I'm short?" It sounded harsh despite Ankh's even tone.

"Of course not! It's because you know electronics and what should or shouldn't be there."

"Okay." Ankh bent down to look under the vehicle.

Rivka nodded and held her hand out to show how tall the Crenellian was.

Once Ankh gave the all-clear, Red climbed in. Jay slid the side door open. "Hang on," Red told her. "Why don't you guys stay clear until after it's running? I mean, put a building between this thing and yourselves."

"You heard the man," Rivka told them. Lindy didn't want to leave. "It'll be fine. This is for Red's peace of mind, not ours. Ankh didn't find anything, and we all trust him, don't we?"

They trooped to the other side of the parking area. *All clear,* Rivka passed.

They couldn't tell that the vehicle was running until Red drove it erratically toward them.

"Maybe we are safer out here," Lindy ventured. The hover-van settled near them, and the side door popped.

"All aboard!" Red shouted from the driver's seat.

They reluctantly climbed in. Once they were inside, Red drove without issue, staying in the travel corridors while Ankh worked his magic to ensure traffic control favored their route. When they reached the spaceport, Red maneuvered around the side of the arrivals terminal and accessed the parking area directly using the Magistrate's carte blanche. They left the van next to *Peacekeeper* and climbed aboard.

Rivka immediately sequestered herself on the bridge and called Grainger.

Fifteen minutes later, Lindy had showered and changed

into something that didn't have dried blood all over it. Everyone ate something, too, except the Magistrate, who was still behind a closed door.

"She's pretty mad," Jay ventured.

"She got her man, but didn't, and then she was prevented from closing the case. I've never seen her not resolve a case. It has to chap her ass," Red added.

"There is more case," Ankh said. The others turned to listen. "Erasmus and I planted tracking programs on the communication tendrils leading from our original message. There is a channel that's still active."

Lindy and Red looked at each other, jaws clenched as they became angry with the local law enforcement.

"Bureaucrats," Red said under his breath.

Jay said what needed to be said. "The Magistrate was right. There's more than one killer."

Red hurried to the bridge and banged on the hatch before opening it. The Magistrate was pacing, and the High Chancellor was on the screen. "Is that you, Vered?" the older gentleman asked, looking past the bodyguard.

"Lindy is dressed this time," Red answered, mouth open to continue. The High Chancellor interrupted, speaking quickly.

"That's not what I was looking for." The man's hands appeared on his screen as if trying to avoid a fight.

Red smiled. "I'm surprised you wouldn't. I can't stop looking myself, but I need to interrupt you for a word with the Magistrate." Rivka had stopped walking and stood with her hands behind her back. "Ankh says that one of the comm channels that supported the killer is active. The shooter wasn't working alone."

"Are we confirmed that there's another? An active broadcast isn't enough hard evidence to pull the case back from the locals. The guy they have in custody is a murderer. But did he commit *all* the murders? I don't think so, since Ankh is starting to paint the picture of a conspiracy. I need something a little more solid to wrest the case back into Federation hands."

"What the locals giveth, the locals taketh away," the High Chancellor pontificated. "Deliver hard evidence of a second suspect and you can wrest jurisdiction back, but not before. What are you most concerned about?"

Rivka turned to the screen. Wrinkles appeared on her forehead as she shaped her feelings into words. "I'm afraid they are going to put a man to death and the murders won't stop. They'll lose face. We'll lose face, and most importantly, innocents will lose their lives."

"Your heart is as big as the galaxy itself, Magistrate Rivka Anoa. This is a delicate stage, since the Federation cannot be heavy-handed regarding a member planet's internal affairs. You may have found the suspect, but how they handle it now is their business. Take care, Rivka. I look forward to seeing how you did what was in the best interest of both Collum Gate and the Federation." The screen faded to black.

Rivka headed for the rec room, pausing to place a friendly hand on Red's shoulder and smile at him. She wasn't sure she'd be able to win this one, but it wouldn't be for the lack of trying.

"C'mon, Red. We have lives to save."

The hover-van raced from the spaceport, Red driving like his hair was on fire. Rivka's team hung on tightly. Red yelled over his shoulder. "They say one hundred and ten kilometers per hour is the speed at which even the best sniper can't hit the target."

"That's also the speed where humans turn into pancakes if you hit something," Rivka shouted back. "What does your anti-assassination manual say about driving with the windows open?"

"I only have the clear ones open, and none of them are bullet-proof, laser refractive, or shielded, so it's a moot point." Red jerked the vehicle through three dimensions, keeping a clear lane ahead for as far as possible.

Ankh threatened to drop a few red lights in Red's way if he didn't slow down.

"That would be bad, Ankh!" Red laughed almost maniacally.

"Did you know he was like this?" Rivka asked out the side of her mouth.

Lindy shook her head. "I should have suspected. Driving is one big competition, and he hates to lose."

"It's not really a competition," Rivka replied helplessly.

"*We* know that..." Lindy left the implication where it was.

Red laughed from deep within his broad chest. He continued to change travel lanes as necessary to maintain the momentum. When he arrived at the Forum, he finally slowed. Ambassadors and other alien delegates were already arriving.

After they were notified that the meeting had been

compromised, they hadn't canceled it, as Rivka had wished. They'd doubled down and moved it forward in time.

The Magistrate jumped from the van while it was settling to the ground. "Catch her!" Red shouted into the back. Lindy pulled herself past Jay and Ankh, dived out the door and sprinted after Rivka. The last two passengers climbed out, Jay hovering protectively over the Crenellian.

Red lowered the hover-van to the ground and bolted from it, locking it as he ran.

"Hold up!" Lindy called when she caught up with the Magistrate. Rivka continued to walk quickly, stomping her feet in aggravation with each new step. "If a murderer is around here, running into the open isn't the best way to let Red and me do our jobs. Let us protect you, Magistrate. At least let us try."

Rivka slowed and let Lindy get beside her. Red flowed to the other side, and they continued toward the indoor amphitheater called the Forum. Jay and Ankh rushed after them, but the Crenellian wasn't good at running. His pace resembled that of an old man trying to use a broken walker.

Jay wasn't strong enough yet to carry him while running. She cursed herself for self-indulgence when she should have been preparing for the next battle like Red and Lindy. Hell, like everyone but her. She was instantly ashamed, and the adrenaline strengthened her resolve not to hold the team back. She hoisted the dense alien and jogged toward the others. She was out of breath when she reached them at the doors.

Red was arguing with the guard. Rivka was trying to get out from behind him to state her case on why they had to let her in. Red finally stepped to the side, even though he was prepared to butt-stroke the guard and remove him from their path.

"I am a Federation Magistrate on Federation business," she declared. He didn't bother checking the screen to see if she was an invitee. She held up her credentials, which listed her in the same capacity as a head of state. She prided herself on being able to talk her way into places, saving her creds for when her powers of persuasion failed.

"Fine," the guard replied, trying to sound bored. "But you can only bring one lackey."

Rivka raised a hand before Red could pummel the man.

"All of them. My entourage is indispensable, and they will all accompany me. You understand that my credentials grant me complete latitude in bringing my party with me."

"Just one." The guard insisted.

"You are now in violation of Federation Law regarding diplomats. I refer you to Appendix D, Chapter Seven, Section 1. The punishment isn't harsh, but you are preventing me from performing my duties. This will hurt me more than you," she promised.

"What are you going to do?" He planted his feet shoulder-width apart and crossed his arms over his chest.

With the speed that her nano-enhancements allowed, she kneed him in the groin, lifting him off the ground. When he touched down, he crumpled, turning into a puddle on the ground like ice cream on Keome.

"You have been judged," Rivka declared.

"She warned you, dumbass." Red was more to the point.

"One more thing." Rivka leaned close, appreciating the tears running from the clenched eyes of the moaning man.

"Make sure no one enters after us. I believe there is going to be an attack."

She swayed past on her way to the interior, where the team found at least a hundred people.

"We need to get them all out of here if you think there's going to be an attack. You're thinking bomb, aren't you?" Red's eyes darted around the area, looking for optimal points to place an explosive. He scoured the rafters for balloons of poison gas, and next were recesses where a bomb could be hidden behind ad hoc projectiles.

"It's too big, Magistrate. We can't search this place without it taking all night." Red moved in front of the Magistrate, offering his body to absorb the impact should there be an explosion.

"We're in this together, Red," Rivka stated, gently pushing past her bodyguard. He followed closely. Lindy, Jay, and Ankh joined them. "No, you guys get out of here!"

"That's not how it works." Jay's resolve rang through her words. "We go where you go."

"I don't have time to argue, but when we get back to the ship, we're going to iron this out."

"I look forward to being alive to go back to the ship," Jay replied.

Lindy winked at her before taking in the crowd. Heads were starting to turn toward the noisy newcomers. The crowd engaged in a low din of hushed voices as they waited for the meeting to start. Fifteen minutes.

Rivka walked toward the dais in the center of the Forum where two alien ambassadors looked out upon the crowd. A humanoid wore gaudy robes of scarlet and gold, while the other was a four-legged Yollin. He stood near the lectern at the side of the dais and watched Rivka approach. She vaulted onto the stage and he flinched, taking a half-step back.

The diplomatic community reacted best to credentials, so she removed hers and flashed them to the ambassadors who appeared to be running the show. Red motioned for Jay and Ankh to start checking around the dais and Lindy positioned herself on the other side of the hall, watching for anything untoward or anyone acting oddly.

She discovered quickly that in a crowd of a hundred different species, there was no standard of odd that she could reconcile. She started looking for the squat humans who made up the population of Collum Gate.

Aliens weren't the threat.

Rivka covered the microphone with her hand before she started speaking. "You're in danger."

"Didn't they catch the killer?" the Yollin ambassador asked.

"One of them. I'm convinced there's a second member of the operation, the one responsible for the bomb. This place is a prime target, and we need to move everyone out; scatter them so we can check the building. I need everyone to return to their embassies or official residences, and I need them to be out of this building in less than ten minutes."

She checked the time on her datapad.

"Eight minutes," Rivka corrected.

"But they caught the killer," the Yollin repeated.

"We caught *one* killer, the shooter. We did not catch the bomber or the stabber. Whether that is one or two people, we don't yet know. You have my word on that as a Federation Magistrate." Rivka was pretty sure, and she was willing to put her creds on the line if that was what it took to convince the aliens to leave the Forum in the next eight minutes. She uncovered the mic. "We can discuss it later, but we need everyone to leave this building right now. And I mean *right now*. I think there is a bomb in here! I hope I'm wrong, but in any case, you need to get out!"

She finished by yelling into the microphone and pointing toward the exits. The ambassadors stood almost as one but moved without a sense of urgency. Since most were elder statesman, their pace was understandable, but Rivka needed them to regain a spark of youth.

"Red." She pointed toward a clear spot on the ceiling. "A little enticement, please."

The crack of hypersonic darts blasting through the overhead lit a fire under the elder statesmen assigned to Collum Gate. The rush cascaded into a stampede, but the ambassadors found kindness in lending a hand to each other as they streamed toward the exits.

"And you, too," she told those on the dais as she waved them toward an exit. They both reluctantly nodded and strolled away.

"Pack it up. Time for us to go," Red ordered, motioning to Ankh and Jay.

"We need to find the device!" Rivka jumped from the dais and joined Ankh in searching where a thing could be hidden. Red stormed over to Rivka, picked her up, and started running. "Come on!" he bellowed.

Rivka fought him for a moment but stopped. "I'll go. Put me down." He slowed and let her feet touch. She nodded as she sprinted toward the door, catching up with the last of the diplomats heading out. Jay scooped up Ankh and struggled to run without the adrenaline surge.

Lindy materialized, taking the Crenellian into her arms, letting her railgun bounce on its sling over her shoulder. Relieved of her burden, Jayita was able to keep pace with the much bigger and stronger bodyguard. Jay's platinum-blue hair was the last through the door. It closed behind her, and despite everyone's expectation, there was no building-destroying explosion.

Once outside, Rivka angled toward the groups that congregated outside. "Don't bunch up!" she yelled at them, waving her arms wildly. Whether they finally got the message or just wanted to avoid the crazy woman, Rivka achieved her desired result. The ambassadors drifted toward their waiting vehicles and departed slowly but surely.

When Rivka checked her datapad, it was ten minutes beyond when the meeting was supposed to start.

"That's not what I expected," she said. Red and Lindy both shrugged. "Maybe it is set for later? Or maybe there is no bomb." Rivka's features fell as dejection set in.

Ankh spoke softly. "Erasmus used the building's wireless electronics to create a sensory screen, blocking all signals into and out of the building."

"As in, if it was a remote activation, it wouldn't have gone through." Rivka was about to tell Ankh to lift the block, but the Yollin ambassador approached. She held up a finger. *Wait one.*

"Madame Magistrate, I have to protest the discombobulation of my meeting. You've singlehandedly set back my place in this group by a hundred years. It will take two life-times to get it back. You've destroyed my credibility!"

The Yollin's mandibles clacked with his agitation.

Rivka looked at Ankh and nodded. "Lift it."

With a crack of lightning and the roll of thunder, windows shattered and the center of the Forum collapsed.

"You were saying?"

Rivka and her team headed for the hover-van.

CHAPTER FOURTEEN

"Take us to the station. I need to talk with the asshole," Rivka said, ice crystals hanging from her words.

"Which one?" Jay wondered. Rivka winced. She wasn't enamored of any of the locals.

Emergency vehicles screamed in alarm as they passed on their way to the Forum, where they would find no casualties. Not even the guy she'd kneed. He had staggered through the parking area the second he'd caught sight of her, trying to put as much distance as possible between his privates and the Magistrate.

"The guvna. I need access to the prisoner." Rivka looked at her datapad, trying to formulate the questions that would lead her to the shooter's accomplice. "Turn the zombie loose."

Ankh shook his big head. Hovering over his small neck, the movement threatened to topple him. "You're not going to like this."

"What?" she asked, already expecting the worst.

"Datapad."

She was holding it in her hands. The screen jumped and shifted. "Did you hack into my pad?"

"Not as far as you know," Ankh delivered in his naturally deadpan voice. Jay chuckled.

"Oh, shit!" Rivka exclaimed. "Step on it, Red. They're going to execute him."

She turned her attention back to the pad, riveted by the scene on the screen. The shooter was chained to a wall while a masked officer stood at ease with the rifle.

"Ankh, contact the station for me and order them to halt the execution. The bombing of the Forum is the evidence I need to reestablish Federation jurisdiction over this case."

Ankh held steady and stared out the front window. Red bumped a girder and nipped another vehicle in his headlong rush toward the station, continuing to accelerate. The traffic lights flashed red and he dodged upward, skipping over the lateral traffic and returning to the travel lanes.

"Come on, buddy. I need those lights."

"They have changed the codes. Reestablishing control now." The last series of lights flared green and held steady. "The station has refused your request to stay the execution."

"Why did they think it was a request?"

"They deemed it so in their denial. It was clear that it was a Federation-based order."

Rivka ground her teeth as she watched the execution theatrics move toward their inevitable conclusion. A microphone appeared before the condemned man. "Any last words?" a voice off-screen asked.

"Fate has already delivered my sentence. I have become the destroyer of worlds, without remorse, without shame. My cause is noble, a purpose far greater than the small minds here can contemplate. A destroyer is a creator when from the ashes, something new arises. Collum Gate had lost its way, but now the people have a chance for redemption, free from external influence. In that, I am the creator of a new and better world. My life is sacrificed for the greater good, and my time now ends because my job is done. Let the new world blossom."

The shooter smiled and faced the camera, appearing to look directly into Rivka's eyes. The microphone disappeared and the camera zoomed out, panning to a single officer, holding the rifle that Red had hoisted from the attic trap. A drum beat three times and stopped. The officer squeezed the trigger and the rifle bucked, but there was no flash or smoke.

The convict jerked once, and his head flopped sideways. The sound had been turned off so viewers wouldn't hear the shot that exploded through the man's chest.

The camera panned out to show the guvna with a firm stance, head held high. Someone shoved a microphone into his face.

"The laws of Collum Gate are sacrosanct in that violence begets violence," the guvna said solemnly in his prepared comments following the execution. "Don't be violent and you won't be on the receiving end of such terrible punishment as we had to witness today. I have to thank Supra Harpeth and his team for finding the criminal and bringing him to Justice. If you have any questions, I'll take those now."

A reporter up front in the small crowd was first to raise her hand. He pointed at her.

"If the executed man was the shooter, then who blew up the Forum at the time of a diplomatic gathering?"

Rivka pointed at the screen. "Answer *that*, asshole!"

The guvna looked over his shoulder to summon the supra, and they talked in hushed tones behind their hands. When he turned back, the guvna raised his arms to quiet the crowd. "I will be looking into that personally. Thank you for coming."

The leader of the local law enforcement walked past those standing with him on the small stage, shaking their hands briefly before he and the entourage hurried off-screen. A commentator's face appeared and started rehashing what had been said, his take on their take on the so-called facts. Nothing new. She tapped her datapad off.

"Why are we going to the law enforcement center again?" Red asked.

"Slow down, Red. I need time to think." Rivka looked out the window and mouthed words but didn't say anything. Red pulled to the side, stopping at a mini-mart.

"Jay, can you run in and buy us some water?" Lindy asked. Red nodded and popped the side door. Jay held her hand out. Lindy was hesitant to give her a credit chip. Ankh put his small hand in hers and climbed out. Together they walked toward the mini-mart.

"Are they, you know..." Lindy wondered.

"No. Crenellians aren't compatible with humans. I think he trusts her, compared to us, who are just oversized barbarians. She put herself between the shooter and him, proving her loyalty with actions, not words. And she's nice all the time, no matter what. Who *wouldn't* want to be her friend?"

"I can't blame him or her. I'm glad you two found each other." Rivka looked up from her datapad. "I think this is going to be a lonely job. We have each other. The locals who should appreciate our help are against us almost as much as the criminals. It chaps my ass. They want our help, but they don't. They want the problem to go away and us to leave their planet. I'm not sure my ass has ever been as chapped as it is right now."

"We'll take your word for it," Red replied. Lindy smiled at him.

Jay opened the minimart's door and held it for Ankh. He strolled out at his slow pace. He looked around as he walked, taking in the sights but unaffected by the grandeur. Jay waved a bag that was stuffed to bursting.

When they reached the hover-van, she passed out bottles of water and see-through baggies with a variety of items best described as nuts, berries, and weeds.

"What am I looking at?" Red asked while examining the bag.

"The clerk called them snack packs, high in energy and nutrition," Jay replied happily. She opened her bag and popped a handful into her mouth. Her smile melted into a sour face. She leaned out the window. Upon seeing the immaculate ground, decided not to spit it out. She hid the bag in her lap as she ejected the foul concoction, closed the baggie and stuffed it all back into the bag.

She held the bag open for her teammates to deposit their snack packs.

"Why is everyone looking at me?"

Rivka shrugged. The respite and camaraderie had cleared her head, and she made a decision. "Take us to the station, Red. I need to talk with Harpeth and the guvna if he'll deign to see me. Ankh, what kind of chatter are we hearing on the diplomatic channels? Are they lining up to leave?"

"Why do you think I know what is happening on the diplomatic channels? They are encrypted."

Rivka stared at him without blinking. He maintained his composure for only a few heartbeats before coming clean.

"Fine. Yes. No one is leaving, but the Yollin ambassador has filed a complaint with Collum Gate about the failure to provide adequate security for the diplomats. He demanded that the Federation take control of the situation. He named you as the only one on this planet who seemed to care about the diplomats. The complaint and demand were signed by over one hundred others, and have been formally registered with the Federation."

"When were you going to tell me this?" Surprise gripped her features as she glared at the Crenellian.

Her datapad registered an incoming call.

"High Chancellor Wyatt." Rivka smiled. "To what do I owe this honor?"

He dipped his head to give her the schoolmarm look.

"Is it about the diplomatic letter?"

He tapped his nose with a finger. "Don't execute any of their bureaucrats. They don't know any better, but you need to take charge of the investigation and find those responsible."

"We nailed one of the bastards, but Collum Gate took him away before I could interrogate him. Then they wouldn't let me see him, as you already know. The explosion at the meeting was what I needed to reestablish jurisdiction over the case, but they refused to comply with my order to stop the execution. I'm pretty miffed," she admitted.

"Cool and calculating—that's what they need. There will be some turmoil at the station since the planet's leadership is now fully involved. I would be surprised if a bunch of people have not already been fired."

"We're on our way there, High Chancellor." Rivka frantically waved at Red to get going. The hover-van lifted off the ground and raced into traffic. The Magistrate hung on as the erratic maneuvers began afresh. She tried to sit still but found it to be impossible. "I'll take care of it. The locals are tools to help me find the shooter's partners."

"They already executed the criminal?" the High Chancellor interrupted. "He had only been in custody for a couple hours."

"They don't mess around. They perform executions using the murderer's own weapon."

"Who are executions for, Magistrate?" Wyatt asked in a patient voice.

"Reduce the burden on society of long-term incarceration of an incorrigible. Communities can't take the risk of a psychopath being reintroduced."

"While you're solving this case and after you've meted out Justice, get back to me with the right answer of why Collum Gate employs capital punishment. And listen to the question. I asked *who* they were for, not what." The High Chancellor's image disappeared, to be replaced by the diplomats' formal complaint. Wyatt had given Rivka homework in the middle of a high-profile case.

She had regurgitated her law school answer, one of many options, but the one she believed. The High Chancellor hadn't bought it. It made her think outside the boundaries of a conspiracy to murder alien diplomats. From her datapad, the official complaint stared at her.

It was worded simply, but the impact had to roil the highest levels of Collum Gate's government.

"Be careful what you ask for, Magistrate. You may get it." Jay was being her honest self. Rivka had wanted jurisdiction in a bad way—and now she had it.

"No one else can die," Rivka punched her fist into her palm. "Ankh! Find me another breadcrumb."

Harpeth rushed out the front door and started running. Rivka held out her hand. *Stop.* The supra slowed to a walk.

"Anything you need, Magistrate, let me know."

"We need a solid forensic examination of the Forum."

"That's where I'm headed now. I invite you to join me?" The supra started inching away.

"I want to talk to the guvna first. We'll meet you there."

"The guvna is inside, but he'll be leaving soon."

"Then we'd better catch him before he goes."

Ankh climbed out of the hover-van. "Are we going to ride with you?" the Crenellian asked, looking at Harpeth.

Jay appeared at Ankh's side, giving the supra the hairy eyeball. Red remained in the driver's seat.

"Lindy, go with them. Red and I will be along as soon as possible." Rivka's stone-cold tone suggested her decision was final. Lindy slugged the last of her water and threw the empty container back in the van. Rivka issued one final warning to the supra. "Listen to my people and take care of them."

Harpeth toed the ground and shuffled his feet. Rivka waited for him to say what he had to say.

"I'm sorry, Magistrate. This has been a goat rope from the first murder. We didn't believe it was orchestrated, and then all of a sudden it was. Then the aliens came down on us for not doing our jobs, while also not helping us. It was like beating our heads against a stone wall when we tried to talk to them. Then you showed up, ran around our city, killed some people, and found the perp. We wanted so badly for it to be over that we didn't hear what you had to say. Thank you for remaining on the case while we were busy patting each other's backs."

"Why did you do that? Collum Gate took all the credit, but we won together. Your people conducted the raids to secure the hideouts, but without him," Rivka pointed to Ankh, "we wouldn't have found any of those places."

"The senior positions are put through a public approval process. We have to uphold the law, but we have to maintain good public relations as well. It prevents heavy-handed law enforcement."

"You mean it prevents *effective* law enforcement. We were looking for a serial killer, and you wanted to pussy-foot around because the public might not approve? How happy are they going to be when they have to pay for the building that was just blown up by the perp you dutifully ignored?" Rivka closed on the supra.

"I can only say I'm sorry so many times. What do you want from me? A resignation? Fine. I failed spectacularly. I should go."

"Stop!" Rivka put all the weight of her position into that one word. "You're going to make this right by getting to the Forum and finding evidence that we can use to corner this scumbag. On the way there keep unfucking yourself, so that you can do your damn job when you arrive!"

Red appeared at Rivka's side as she stormed toward to the station's entrance. The hover-van was abandoned in the middle of the lot, but no one was going to mess with it.

"Shall we?" Jay offered, motioning for the supra to lead the way to his vehicle.

"Are you that mad?" Red asked, not looking at Rivka as he scoured the station's main entry for threats. There were enough uniforms inside that he was not very concerned. He would never be completely at ease, except inside *Peacekeeper*. He thought the name fit.

"Nah. I wanted him to stop his waffley bullshit and get to work. Someone who knows how to make sophisticated bombs is out there. Every person in this city is at risk, and Harpeth knows the ins and outs of how things work. He also has access to resources we need, like people and labs." Rivka looked up at her bodyguard. "I remember a time not that long ago when a certain man mountain would have said that such things weren't his concern."

"Times change. When cases became missions, we evolved into a combat squad where we all have to watch each other's backs. It's not that I didn't care about this stuff before, but that my job was different. And what I do today is different from what I did back then. Did you see Jay shielding Ankh with her body? Jay. She gave you the finger, and you almost ripped it off her hand. Now she's protecting the smart guy with the big head and stupid goggles."

Rivka chuckled softly. "I am blessed with a great team. We better get in there before the guvna escapes. Plus, I need to talk to the other five suspects, assuming they haven't executed them or let them go already."

They started to walk toward the elevator, and officers got out of their way. The word had already been passed. Don't mess with the Magistrate.

Once on the elevator, Rivka turned toward Red. "There's a price on your head, isn't there?"

The large man wasn't surprised that she knew. He nodded.

"What do you say when we're finished here, we find your former employers and have a conversation? I think afterward, you and my other bodyguard will be safe to take a nice vacation somewhere. A place you can go without your weapons and maybe let your hair down."

Red bumped his helmet off and ran a hand over his smoothly shaven head. "I'd like that. I'd like to see those two punished for their crimes, but you won't get testimony from me. I gave them my word, and you know how I feel about that. They're scumbags, but it'll take you all of ten seconds to learn that on your own."

"We'll take care of them, Red. You, me, Lindy…all of us. We're going to ruin their day."

"They won't know what hit them." Red smiled, but his eyes turned dark and dangerous.

On their floor, the Magistrate led the way toward the guvna's office. Perps and field hands didn't pollute this floor of the facility. It was immaculate, and decorated better than the palaces on some planets.

"Methinks they aren't a slave to their budget like most police forces. Too much success and the politicos start cutting funding," Rivka mumbled as she walked through the outer office, ignoring the assistant at the desk outside the massive doors leading to the inner chamber. Rivka shook her head as she ground her teeth, yanked the door open, and headed in.

The guvna stiffened when he saw her. A box on the desk was stuffed with a number of personal items. The room looked like it had been sanitized.

Rivka didn't beat around the bush. "Why did you execute that man?"

"He committed a capital crime under Collum Gate law. Everything was done in accordance with the law." The guvna sounded like he was parroting a media release.

"But not in accordance with common sense. The case wasn't closed. I told you that!" she growled. She didn't know what answer he could give that would satisfy her. Maybe she only needed her pound of flesh.

He didn't reply. Nothing he said would have been good enough.

There was no value in further words with the guvna. In less than a day, he had gone from being an ally to an obstacle to a fading image in Rivka's rearview mirror. "Where are the suspects from the raids?"

"Two floors down," he replied softly. Rivka turned and left. Red glared briefly before following her out.

CHAPTER FIFTEEN

Rivka was given access to the suspects, four men and one woman, without question. She visited them in their cells, not wanting to waste time by having them moved to an interrogation room.

"What were you doing in that house?" she asked each while holding an arm. Some tried to fight, but they weren't strong enough. Nowhere *near* strong enough. Red loomed nearby, which helped reduce their spirits.

Four were squatters, but the last one, the woman, was quiet and confident.

"What were you doing in that house?"

The woman's arm remained limp as images flitted across Rivka's mind. It was like watching the heat shimmer over a desert's sands. Watching. Waiting for the right time. Aliens!

"Describe what was going to happen at the right time?" Rivka asked.

"Very good. You can see into my mind. How about

this?" the woman said projecting lurid images of her and a naked Red.

Rivka let go and stepped backward. The woman lunged forward despite her handcuffs and grabbed Rivka's hand to continue pummeling her with warped images of gratuitous sex.

Red peeled the suspect's hand off the Magistrate's arm and slammed her back into the chair. "Stay down!" he ordered, moving behind her and waiting.

"If *you* only would stay down," she purred.

"I don't know what she's doing, Magistrate, but you're better than her. Work through it and find out what you need to know."

Rivka met Red's eyes. He dipped them to point at the woman. Rivka surged into her, grabbing both wrists. "Who are you working with?"

The images bounced. A face appeared. A man, shrouded in shadows as he talked in a low voice. Naked people!

"What's his name?" Rivka pressed, squeezing the woman's wrists and yanking her arms.

She didn't know his name, but he worked at the *Collum Daily*. He was sitting in a cool room filled with equipment, showing the woman around. His face became clear under the lights.

Rivka had seen him in the building.

"Let's go!" She pushed the woman away and stepped to the door. The woman tried to get up, but Red dropped a hammer fist on top of her head, crunching her neck and driving her into her seat. She collapsed over the table before sliding to the floor.

In the hallway, Rivka grabbed the waiting guard. "The

other four are free to go, but that one, she's an accomplice. Lock her up, but whatever you do, *don't kill her!*"

Rivka ran to the elevator.

"Where to, Magistrate?" Red inquired.

"The *Collum Daily*."

"Can't this thing go any faster?" Lindy asked. The driver ignored her. Harpeth leaned over his shoulder.

"Uniforms, both lostas and petros, are already on the scene and have the area cordoned off. An analysis van is on its way. Manpower to sift the wreckage is being assembled. Getting there a few minutes sooner isn't worth the risk." Harpeth hesitated before adding, "In my opinion."

Lindy nodded. Ankh stared out the front window, lost in communing with his AI. Jay watched the people and their body language. She wanted to do more for the team. She hadn't done anything to help this case, including buying something that was a cross between dead squid rotting on the beach and fermented cabbage—snacks purchased with Ankh's credit chip because hers was maxed out.

She bowed her head and tried not to cry.

Lindy started rubbing her shoulders. "It's okay," she whispered. Jay wore her emotions on her sleeve, so there was no doubt she was upset. Lindy understood why because she also hadn't contributed much on this case, not in her mind anyway. She started to laugh. Jay turned, her anger fighting her sorrow.

"I was thinking about how little I've done for the

Magistrate today, but then I remembered. I got to body-slam that one bitch who sold out her people to be the queen of the news."

Jay smiled. "Yeah, you did. Ass over teacups."

"While we're occupied guarding the Magistrate, you've been watching over Ankh. It may not seem like a lot, but he's the one they shot at."

"I know. If you ever wondered, now you know. The Magistrate would take a bullet for any of us. As would Red. I wonder if I will. I'd like to think so. I know you will. And Ankh will use his techno-magic to save us all."

The big, bald head turned, goggles firmly in place on his forehead. "It's not magic, it's mastery. Some work with the technology, having a rudimentary understanding of the science, and others, like Ted, bend it to their will."

"Profound, Ankh," Lindy stated.

"I'm afraid I would only block a bullet destined to hit you in the kneecap, and that's not a good use of my life, but I am working on a personal shield. With further miniaturization of an Etheric power supply, I believe I can build something that would protect us all."

"Raise shields, Number One!" Lindy said in her huskiest voice. Jay looked confused again. "It's some stupid video series that Red watches."

"I bet he doesn't think it's stupid," Ankh postulated.

"No. And don't you tell him I said that!"

Ankh looked at Lindy with his usual blank expression. They both jumped when the door popped up. They'd arrived at the Forum, and it was a beehive of activity.

Red couldn't drive like he wanted to. Without Ankh, they didn't have a straight shot of green lights. It seemed to be the opposite, stopping at each intersection to wait for the traffic. The Magistrate was in the back. Even though she'd wanted to be up front, Red had talked her out of it.

She played with her datapad. "Chaz, show me a layout of the building. Where is the computer room?"

"The basement," the evolved EI replied. A map with arrows showed the way. At the back side of the stairs that commanded the main floor was the stairway down.

"Why are they always in the basement? What the hell is up with that?"

"It's a tactically inferior position," Red replied, drumming his fingers on the driver's yoke while waiting for the light to change. "But it's easier to keep cooler."

"You'd think that with modern technology, those things could be smaller and better cool themselves."

"Every time technology advances we want more of it, and content expands to fill new capacity. The newest stuff is more powerful than ever, as is the demand."

"Where did Red go?" Rivka punched her bodyguard in the arm. "I'll buy your explanation."

"Do you think he'll be there?" Red asked.

"No. I think he left the second we launched Miss Prissy Pants out the door. Do you have any of Ankh's coins?"

"Two. Didn't you stock up when we were back on the ship?"

"I forgot." Rivka shrugged. "Ain't no 'I' in team." She pushed on Red's shoulder, but he didn't budge. There was too much of him and too little space in the driver's seat.

"Ain't no Ankh coins either, Magistrate."

When they finally hovered into the parking area, they found the lot mostly empty of personal vehicles.

Red climbed out, stretching as his eyes searched. He reached back in to get his railgun. Rivka opened the side door, making Red rush around the vehicle.

"You think they packed it in for the day?" Red asked.

They hurried to the main entrance, happy to find it unlocked.

"I think they work early hours. Maybe this is normal for the late afternoon in the digital publishing world before the night shift comes in to set everything up for the next day."

They found minimal staffing, but they didn't care about the journalists or paper pushers. Their target was IT, information technology. They went around the main staircase and down, finding the computer room at the bottom. Inside, a young woman was at the desk working on a programming issue using a holographic interface. She almost jumped out of her skin when Rivka poked her shoulder. She fumbled with the physical controls until the holoscreens dropped.

"Who are you?" she demanded.

"I'm Magistrate Rivka. There's a man who works here..."

"There are a lot of men who work here. You'll have to be more specific."

Rivka took a slow breath. She pointed to the workstation where she'd seen him in the suspect's mind. "He was sitting right there. Brown hair, a little spikey, not too tall. What's his name?"

The woman knew who she was talking about. Recognition flashed across her features before she tried to put on a brave face.

"What's his name?" Rivka asked as she gently touched the woman's small shoulder.

She recoiled, but not before the name appeared in her mind.

"Bindola Shnobhauer. Really?"

"I didn't say anything!" the woman protested.

"Now you're afraid. Why? You know he's killing people, and you believe that if he thinks you gave him up, he's going to come after you."

"I didn't know, but he's creepy. Who isn't, down here?" She took in the entirety of the space with a grand gesture. She sat down and buried her head in her hands.

"What else do you know that will help us find him? Please understand that I won't rest until we've caught him. He left early today, before the end of his shift, didn't he?"

She nodded reluctantly, blinking rapidly.

"Where can we find him?"

"I don't know. I don't hang out with the guy. He's creepy, always making remarks about aliens doing weird stuff."

Rivka checked Bindola's workstation. She held out a hand, and Red placed one of Ankh's devices into it. She put it behind the flashing systems. As usual, all the computers were operating.

Ankh, I think we found our bomber's name. Bindola Shnobhauer. I've put one of your devices on the workstation that he was using. Get this... Rivka passed over their internal comm link.

He worked at the Collum Daily, *Ankh finished.*

If you knew that, why didn't you tell me?

I can't share every half-baked notion I have. I had no evidence besides a hunch based on how the broadcast signal traveled. It wasn't really broadcast, simply sent unidirectionally.

How was it half-baked if it was right? Never mind. Can you access his system and dig out any information on where he might be or what his next target may be?

Rivka waited impatiently. "Have I become so spoiled by the speed with which Ankh does things that when something takes longer than five seconds, I want to start pounding on the desk?"

"He is good, but yes, you've been spoiled by your team's awesomeness."

"Not a word I would have thought you would use, but I'll take it. Come on, Ankh, tell me you're done." Rivka smiled as if his voice would appear inside her head. It didn't. She grumped and moped around the IT section as she tried to kill time.

When Ankh's voice returned, it carried an unusual sense of urgency. *You must get to the Crenellians' building. There's a car bomb.*

"Car bomb in front of the Crenellian business!" Rivka blurted.

Red didn't hesitate. He flung the door open and raced up the steps. Rivka was right behind him, pushing him to go faster.

"We need to go," Ankh insisted. He started pulling Jay but quickly ran out of energy. "He's going to bomb my people."

"Then that's the last place you need to be," Lindy argued.

"No! I need to help them."

"Help them do what?" Lindy asked. Jay was torn between wanting to help her friend and doing what was right by that very same friend. "If I've learned anything from Red, it's that if you know there's going to be shooting, stay out of the line of fire."

"There's not going to be any shooting. It's a bomb," Ankh retorted.

"Same premise. We're not going. Can't you do your thing from inside the van?" Lindy waved at Harpeth, who was standing knee-deep in rubble nearby. He looked annoyed for a moment before climbing to where Ankh weakly tugged on Jay's hand. "Ankh says there's a bomb at the Crenellian business building."

The supra whipped out his communication device and started issuing orders. When he shut it down, he spoke softly. "Three units are en route to cordon off the area. And that's it. There are no other officers available."

"Can't you call them from elsewhere in the city?" Jay asked.

Harpeth glanced past Lindy, Jay, and Ankh. All around them lay what used to be the Collum Gate's finest conference center. Lights flashed and people moved slowly, checking things and moving on. "There isn't anyone. We aren't staffed for multiple major issues."

"Diplomatic security?" Lindy suggested.

"The Crenellians run a business. They aren't an accredited diplomatic post, so they don't rate security."

"Maybe other diplomats can offer their contingents to help?" Lindy urged.

"I won't ask them that. With the murders, and now this? I can't take the risk of asking them to loosen their own security for someone else. Spreading us thin may be the plan. Then they'll hit where we aren't."

Lindy picked up Ankh and starting running toward the police vehicle. "Are we going?" Jay called after them. She followed.

CHAPTER SIXTEEN

Ankh, buddy, give me some green lights, Red begged.

Have the Magistrate send me your route.

"I heard," Rivka said from the back seat. She hunched over her datapad and tapped the map, dragged a finger along the route, and hit Send.

Accessing now. You can accelerate. It'll be green by the time you get there.

Red jammed the accelerator down, and the hover-van leapt forward. He took the highest travel lane. At that speed, he was able to skip over other vehicles, much to the passed drivers' chagrin. Rivka held on, cringing and starting to flinch in anticipation of a collision. The light remained red.

"We're going to die," Rivka proclaimed.

The light changed, and Red hit the intersection at nearly full speed. He barely missed the last of the cross traffic, but the lane ahead was now clear. He took a lower lane, and the vehicle increased speed. It wasn't long before he caught up with the traffic, and he started to swerve and dodge between the vehicles.

Rivka checked her datapad amid the bouncing and jerking. When she kept it even with her eyes, the map showed they were less than five minutes away. She wondered if it was taking into account Red's egregious speed.

She had her answer three minutes later when the van slowed to a crawl to turn the corner onto the street where they would find the Crenellians. Their building, which bordered the diplomatic sector, was an icon of modern architecture, welcoming to locals and aliens alike.

Parked vehicles lined the roadway before it. According to Ankh, one of them contained a bomb. Judging by the destruction at the Forum, they wouldn't be able to use the leased hover-van to block the explosion, but that was what they were going to do anyway.

"Put it right in front of the doorway, Red."

"My thoughts exactly, Magistrate." The hover-van rushed ahead, swerved off the main travel lane, and stopped in front of an ornate building with a simple entrance. Over the double door was a sign that said, Crenellations, Inc. Beneath that was a quote: Secure your planet. Secure your people.

Rivka jumped from the van and up the steps. She tried the door, but it was locked. She pounded on it with one hand, stabbing the buzzer with the other. Red climbed out of the hover-van on the side opposite the parked vehicles. He stood tall right behind the Magistrate, tightening his helmet and blocking as much space around her as his massive frame allowed.

"Come on, people!" Rivka shouted.

"What if Ankh already had them evacuate?"

"Dammit." Rivka turned to her internal comm chip. *Ankh, did you tell the Crenellians to evacuate? We're here, and no one is answering.*

She waited. She felt like her head would explode.

Ankh, buddy, are you there? "Ankh isn't answering."

Lindy, are you with Ankh? Red asked, talking to the whole team.

He's jamming the activation signal like he did at the Forum. It's taking all he's got, it appears. I've never seen a vein throb in his forehead before. I don't know if he warned his people, but you need to get out of there. He looks like he's barely in control.

"Come on!" Rivka yelled, keeping her finger on the buzzer. A Crenellian face appeared on a small screen above the button.

"You can let go of the button now," a voice said, sounding nearly identical to Ankh in the delivery.

"You're in danger. Someone has planted a bomb, and you need to get out. How many of you are in there?"

"What if you're the bomber?" the voice asked.

"Say what? I'm Magistrate Rivka Anoa. Ankh'Po'Turn is on my team, and he is afraid for your safety. Please, come with me."

"We are safe inside, I assure you. *Ankh.* He told us he had arrived. He's an outcast from gentle Crenellian society. He turned on us and is no longer welcome on Crenellia. You need to know who you've cast your lot with."

"I really don't care about any of that. There's a bomb out here, and it'll be best if we're not out here with it."

The screen went blank.

"You have got to be shitting me." Rivka stabbed the buzzer button and held it down. She could hear the tone through the door until it stopped. She pressed the button a few times to confirm her suspicions.

The Crenellians had deactivated the button.

"Fuck those guys," Red said. Rivka nodded, evaluated the situation, and came to a decision. "We can't let their neighbors get blasted. We need to find that bomb."

"No, you don't!" Red declared, grabbing the Magistrate by the arm. "We need to go. Let the bomb techs find it and take care of it."

Rivka shrugged free and pointed up and down the street. "What bomb techs? How long before Ankh loses control? We need to find it and either deactivate it or drag it out of here."

"What do you know about disarming a bomb?" The whites of Red's eyes shone with the passion of his plea.

"I have Chaz at my beck and call. Shall we?" Rivka asked calmly.

"You will be the death of me." Red's shoulders sagged in his surrender to the Magistrate's will.

"But you won't be the death of me." She slapped Red on the shoulder and ran to the first vehicle opposite the door. "I'll go this way, and you go that way."

She peeked through both the front and back windows while trying to see under the skirts of the various hover configurations. She finally moved close, braced her legs, and lifted the vehicle with one arm to look beneath. Fans, wiring, directional controls—nothing untoward.

Red had his hands cupped around his face as he tried to

see into the next vehicle. Once satisfied that it wasn't packed with explosives or unidentified boxes, he followed Rivka's lead in lifting up the vehicle to look underneath. Satisfied that there was nothing obvious, he moved to the next.

Just like Rivka.

And then they moved to the next and the next until they reached the end of the street.

We haven't found anything in any of the vehicles lining the street, Rivka reported to her team. *I hate to ask this, but is Ankh sure it's a vehicle bomb?*

The long delay suggested no one knew.

Anyone have an idea of what we do until Ankh is back with us?

Get Ankh to stop what he's doing, but only after you've cleared out, Lindy replied.

Red and Rivka met back at the van. "What if this was an elaborate ruse?" Rivka asked.

"That guy is more than capable, judging by how hard Ankh has had to work to find the breadcrumbs," Red answered. "I don't know what to tell you, but what if he hid the bomb better than we were able to check?"

"And standing in the open like two morons is not the best way to deal with the lack of evidence?"

"I remain in awe of your eloquence, Magistrate."

She flashed her middle finger at him.

The inaction stalemate was broken by the arrival of a delivery van. The hover-vehicle eased down the street to stop in front of Crenellations, Inc. Rivka waved and Red walked around the other side, his hand on his slung rail-gun, ready to pull it to the front.

The driver watched in alarm. "Can you move your van? I have a delivery for this address."

Rivka smiled at the driver.

"I'm Magistrate Rivka Anoa, and I need to see that package."

"No can do," the man replied, pursing his lips in his belligerence. "On-Time Delivery guarantees that the packages in its care are secure at all times. We have a contract between the sender and the recipient that we hold dear. I'm sorry." His eyes turned to Red who leaned casually against his hover-van with his railgun balanced across both hands.

"You can threaten me, but I won't budge. Fine. I'll carry it around your vehicle."

When Rivka reached through the window to stop the man, he floored it, and she grabbed him by the throat. The vehicle dove forward with Rivka flopping half in and half out of the driver's window. The van jerked to a stop.

"I'm a Federation Magistrate executing a valid search warrant. Don't move this vehicle while I register it with your company. She kept one hand on his throat but stopped squeezing when he clutched at the offending arm. Rivka removed her datapad and balanced it against the window frame. "Chaz, transmit a search warrant to On-Time Delivery that I need to see the package intended for delivery to Crenellations, Inc. Driver is..." She looked purposefully at the driver.

"Number 37. Belesta," he stated.

"Got it?"

"Yes, Magistrate. The warrant has been transmitted."

"Now park this vehicle right here and get out. I think

you're carrying a bomb, so you need to put as much distance between this van and you as you can. I'll let you go as soon as you park it. Do not shut the vehicle off.

The driver tapped it into Park, but kept his hand over the button to re-engage the drive.

"If you do that, I'll have my bodyguard kill you and destroy your vehicle. How does that sound?"

"It sounds like bullshit. Who *are* you people?"

The driver's communication screen lit up with an order from his company to cooperate with Federation authorities.

"It's all you, Magistrate." He released his seatbelt and signed that he was going to get out.

She let go and stepped back for the man to get out. When he opened the door, Red looked disappointed that he didn't get to fire his railgun.

The man started walking, glancing over his shoulder as he went. When the Magistrate carefully opened the back door, he started to run. Rivka dove to the ground. Red ducked behind his hover-van and covered his ears.

Nothing happened.

"I thought he might have been an accomplice," Rivka said. She stood up to find a single package in the back of the delivery vehicle. Red aimed his railgun at the man's back. Rivka waved him off. "Let him go."

"As you wish," Red slung his weapon and joined Rivka in looking at the outside of the package.

"What are you doing?" she asked.

"If you're going to get blown up, it wouldn't do my resume any good to survive the ordeal."

"Fair enough. For the record, I have no intention of

getting blown up."

"For the record, I have absolutely no control over whether you get yourself blown up or not. The least I can do is have my atoms scattered with yours."

"That's so romantic. Do you talk to Lindy that way?"

"She hasn't tried to get me blown up."

Rivka put her hands on her hips and glared at her bodyguard. He pointed at the package with his eyes. "Are you going to open it?"

"I don't think so. What do you say we move the van to the open field, and you light it up with Blazer?"

"Now you're talking my language." He got in, started it, lifted off, and moved the van slowly toward the field. He parked it in the middle and walked a safe distance to a shallow ravine. Rivka joined him, and they dropped behind the hill. With a clean field of fire and nothing behind the van for kilometers. Red smiled, Rivka covered her ears, and he fired.

With precision, he walked the hypervelocity projectiles back and forth through the cargo area of the delivery van.

"You think it should have blown up by now?" Red asked.

Lindy, get Ankh to lift his block. We're clear.

Wait! Red jumped in. "Did you check *our* van? It was parked outside the *Collum Daily* while he was there."

"Dammit! Could we have put it any closer to the building?"

"I don't think so." Red jumped up and started to run. He twisted his arm behind him to point at Rivka, who had popped up behind him. "Stay there!"

Don't lift the block! Just a few more minutes, Rivka

encouraged.

Hurry, Lindy replied.

It took Red four seconds to find the device. Where could someone put a bomb where they wouldn't attract attention? Behind a panel above the skirt in the rear engine compartment. When Red saw it, he quickly shut the panel and ran to the driver's seat. He fired the vehicle up and headed toward the field, skimming over the ground until he could park it next to the delivery van.

He shut it down and ran. Right before he reached the ravine, he gave Rivka the thumbs-up.

Tell Ankh to lift his block.

The explosion was spectacular, reducing their hover-van to a cloud of flying debris and the bottom frame and turning the delivery van into a smoking husk.

"I wonder what was in the package to the Crenellians?" Rivka stood when the debris stopped falling.

"I bet they'll know when something they ordered never arrives. We could say there was a bomb in the package," Red suggested.

"We could. We'll leave it as an open issue. They can make a claim if they so wish, but I don't think they will." Rivka chewed the inside of her lip. "They could have gotten their package, but they were jerks and left us by ourselves to guess what it was."

"Now what?"

"The next breadcrumb. Our perp is on the run in a city with a hundred thousand humans and ten thousand aliens. I'm sure he has a lot of places to hide, so we have to either root him out or draw him out." Rivka nodded definitively. "I think a challenge to his manhood is in order."

CHAPTER SEVENTEEN

When the law enforcement van showed up, Ankh was sound asleep, head cradled in Jay's lap.

"Sorry it took so long to find the bomb," Rivka said softly.

"But we won, right?" Jay replied.

"We stopped him this time, thanks to a little luck. Look what Ankh had to go through to keep us safe. If he hadn't done that, we would have been smears on the facade of Crenellations, Inc."

Red found Lindy and pulled her to him, kissing her deeply. Rivka watched in growing discomfort. "Excuse me. Bomber on the loose."

"I'd say I was sorry, but I'm not," Red started.

"Should we wake him so he can see his fellow Crenellians?" Jay asked.

"No." Rivka slowly shook her head. "They said he was a traitor to his people."

Jay put a hand over the small ear on the side of Ankh's oversized head. "I need to go kick their asses," she declared.

Rivka stopped her with a hand and a smile. "No need. He found his people on the *War Axe*, and then he found us. Can you imagine living in a place where there's no sense of humor?"

Silence filled the van. Jay softly stroked Ankh's head, picking at the night vision goggles that remained propped on his forehead.

"Isn't that the steampunk look?" Red ventured.

"I like it. It's much better than smoking a pipe to look distinguished." Jay smiled at the sleeping alien.

"Where's Harpeth?" Rivka asked.

"Still at the Forum."

"Did they find anything?"

Lindy shook her head. "Not a damn thing."

"I suspect the bombs are self-sanitizing. They blow up in a way that vaporizes the mechanics of the device. For how small they are, they pack a hell of a wallop." Rivka pointed at the front seat, and Red climbed in. "Back to the Forum, my good man!" Rivka called to the driver.

"Yes, Magistrate." The specialist secured the door, lifted off, and headed out.

The pace of the search had slowed by the time the Magistrate returned to the Forum. The last time she had seen it, the dust cloud still hung heavy in the air, and the explosion was ringing in her ears. Supra Harpeth waved for her to follow him to the forensics van.

To Rivka, it looked new, but the supra said it was ten years old but little-used. They didn't often have events of that magnitude. "There was only one other, but that was a building collapse from shoddy workmanship. Otherwise, the lab deploys during the annual exercises. That's it."

Inside, they found it nearly immaculate, with a single aisle and narrow tables with shelves lining both sides and shelves checkerboarding the walls. The technology was arrayed across the front wall. Various devices to scan, sample, and report were stacked for ease of access and use.

A single technician worked while instrumental music played softly in the background. He was examining varied bits and pieces using a magnifying lens attached to eyeglasses. No one wore eyeglasses on Collum Gate. That was old tech. These were specific to the job and probably standard kit for the van. When the technician looked up at the impatiently waiting duo, his bug eyes shot wide.

He removed the glasses and blinked the lights clear. "I didn't hear you come in."

"What's the word?" the supra asked, focusing on the technician and not the myriad of bits and pieces scattered across the tables and shelves.

"I have some interesting bits of wiring, but it could be from anything. That was a big building."

"Nothing, then?" Harpeth sounded dejected.

The technician shook his head. "I'll keep looking. There's a lot more to sort through."

Rivka thanked him before leaving the van.

Twilight was settling over the city. "We could start fresh in the morning," Harpeth offered.

"Or we could keep him running until he messes up. I expect your people are raiding every address known for our Mister Shnobhauer."

"Once this area was isolated and no casualties were confirmed, we sent out three teams. They've found nothing. He cleared out earlier today from his main residence."

"What did he take with him?" Rivka leaned close.

"I don't know," Harpeth admitted.

"Take us there right now, please."

Harpeth pinched his eyes shut, and his face turned pale. "This could be the longest day I've ever had."

"You're kidding? We're going to keep running until we catch him. He's vulnerable at this time, and we're going to take advantage. Put on your big-boy pants. We have work to do." Rivka didn't wait. She walked quickly to the van, nodding to the driver as she shut the side door. Harpeth worked his way into the front seat and announced the address. The law enforcement hover-van lifted into the air and sped away.

Ankh continued to sleep. Red played with his railgun.

"You got to fire it today, so you should be happy."

"I shot up a package filled with bistok bacon."

"How do you know what was in there?" Rivka wondered.

"I'm making stuff up. It's better than Crenellian underpants, which probably look like little kid superhero shorts."

Rivka snorted, happy that Ankh hadn't heard. Jay tried to give him a dirty look, biting her lip to keep from laughing.

"Onward and upward," Rivka stated. "We're going to check the Shnobmeister's house to see what he took with him."

Rivka put down her datapad and started conversing with Chaz. "Let's put him on his heels. We need to enlist the aid of one hundred thousand pairs of eyes. Chaz, plaster his image on every video screen and personal media device in the city. This is a crimson alert for a terrorist on the loose. We are getting closer, which means he becomes more and more like a trapped animal. The big question is, will he sacrifice his life for his cause? If not, then he'll be easier to catch. And once we have him, what are you going to do, Supra Harpeth?"

The supra contorted himself in the front seat to look into the back of the van. He locked eyes with the Magistrate. "We're going to do whatever you agree to. If you want to retain jurisdiction, then so be it. If you want to hand him over to us, we'll have to figure out how to blow him up, assuming the evidence supports his guilt."

"He came after me and my friends. I will confirm what I know, I will judge him, and then I will mete out Justice." Rivka looked back at her datapad. "Broadcast the city-wide search, Chaz. Let's make him crawl into a hole. Supra, have your people ready to respond. I think we're done with the Forum. Extra effort there gains us nothing."

"Roger that, Magistrate." Harpeth used his communication equipment to issue orders to a broad range of law enforcement personnel. When he closed out the last call, he looked satisfied. "Maybe we *will* get some sleep tonight."

"Maybe," Rivka said, not as confidently as Harpeth.

Bindola Shnobhauer lived an austere life. His apartment in an upscale neighborhood lacked decoration. The suspect had gone on the run with whatever he could grab. It was up to Rivka to discover what that was, and how far it could take him.

Red hovered over her as she searched. "Watch out for traps. Maybe you could let me do this?"

"And let you dig in with those meat mallets you call fingers?"

"I'm naturally endowed."

Lindy snickered from the doorway.

"I don't think the Shnob-meister is the trap guy. He blows stuff up, which makes me wonder...where's his bomb factory? It isn't here and was probably never here. Where's his vehicle?"

"Harpeth?" Rivka called. "Is his vehicle included in the city-wide search?"

"He didn't have a vehicle; nothing that we can find, anyway. We're talking with the neighbors to get a description of how he came and went, and especially how he left earlier today."

Rivka thanked him for staying ahead of the investigation, and he went back outside to continue his coordination of the information collection and manhunt.

The Magistrate dug through the dresser and closet trying to figure out what clothes had been taken. A square mark indented into the closet's carpet suggested that a rather large suitcase had been there. She held her hands out to gauge the size. "What do you think he put in here?" she asked.

Red shook his head. "That would hold the whole dresser's worth of clothes, and since the dresser is mostly full, my guess is that it wasn't clothes. Maybe his bomb factory?"

Rivka called for the forensics specialist to sample residue on the floor and wall around where the suitcase had been. If there were any explosives, that was where they would find them. The dining table had already been wiped for trace evidence. Fingerprints on the entry pad and inside the apartment told them that only Bindola had been there.

No visitors.

Rivka put her hands behind her back and started pacing. "A lone bomber. That fits the profile, but he wasn't alone. He was influential enough to convince the shooter to take up his cause, which resulted in the commission of a capital crime. That's pretty significant. So where did this happen? Online in a secret forum somewhere? Ankh and Erasmus would have found that. Where else? Is there a secret anti-alien society?"

She stared at the floor as she tried to find the question that might lead her to the next breadcrumb.

"Whenever I hear someone talk about a secret society," Red started. He didn't finish the thought.

"What?"

"It's bullshit. Everyone lies, and there's a second part to that. No one can keep a secret. Secret societies would be the cool thing to be a part of, but only if people know."

Rivka puffed out her cheeks and sucked them back in as she contemplated what Red had said. "Then where did he meet his partner in crime? And the big question is, how many more are in on it? The pro-alien sentiment here isn't what the government wants you to believe."

Lindy stepped in. "How big is the anti-alien under-ground? Harpeth has to know. He's too smart to be blind to it. The movement may have grown quickly, but that's also its weakness. To grow, there has to be a fertile field and a way to share the seeds."

"I'm surrounded by the *best* people." Rivka smiled at her bodyguards, who were becoming far more than simple security. They'd always been more, but now they were starting to shine brightly.

Her burden of having to see all and know all was getting lighter.

"It is surprising," Lindy continued, "what people say when they're eating and especially drinking. I don't know if they think their server is invisible or if they're trying to impress the server with their deep thoughts, but it happens. If we can find out where he ate, we'll be able to get insight from the workers. They will know something."

"The kitchen suggests he wasn't a big eat-at-home kind of guy. Supra!" Rivka shouted on her way outside. Red and Lindy hurried to catch up and take flanking positions. When Harpeth popped his head out of the van, his hand over his comm device, Rivka continued, "We want to know where Shnobhauer ate. His financial records may provide some insight, but however you can get the information, we need it. There are people we need to talk to."

The station was a bustle of activity. Everyone was doing something, and Supra Harpeth was pulling his hair out. Without the guvna flying top cover, he had to field requests from both above and below him in the chain of command. He was wearing down quickly.

Rivka felt sorry for him, but she had a killer to catch.

After the broadcast went out, the tips started pouring in. The station was inundated.

Harpeth helped himself to another cup of coffee, offering some to Rivka and her team. Inside the law enforcement building, with the new deference paid to the Magistrate, Red and Lindy were still on the job of keeping Rivka safe, but they were able to relax. They both accepted large mugs of steaming java.

Lindy had carried the sleeping Crenellian from the van and put him on the supra's couch. Jay was folded over next to him, also out cold.

Rivka accessed her datapad, and it vibrated. She tapped it, and a familiar voice spoke.

"I have some information for you," Erasmus said.

"You can work while Ankh sleeps? Why didn't I know this?"

"I don't know why you wouldn't know. Ankh doesn't sleep very often or for very long. I always work. I'm an AI. I don't need sleep."

"But you're in his head. Never mind. I appreciate you jumping in to help us."

"It is impossible to tell if the suspect knows that the links from the servers have tracers. The programs are extremely sophisticated. My ego wants to tell me that he'll never find them, but reality dictates that I have to consider the possibility. There are pulls on alien schedules. The Ixtali, the triumvirate of representatives from the Alaxar Trinary, the Yollins, and the planted agenda for the Crenellian ambassador."

The revelation reinforced what Rivka had expected. The bomber would rise to the challenge.

"Send those itineraries to my pad. Is there anything else you can tell us, like where he ate, or if he rented a vehicle?"

"We've sent his image to every rental and leasing agent in the city. No one has replied."

"I suspect that he has dozens of fake profiles. He didn't expect to get caught, but he planned for it, just like he planned for everything else. How is he two steps ahead of everything we do?"

"He could have help, like an AI." Erasmus' voice lingered. Rivka was the first to make a sound when she blew out the breath she'd been holding. "Can we get in front of an AI?"

Erasmus laughed. "Not all AIs are created equal, Magistrate. I will allocate a part of my processes to this question. We *will* get in front of this individual, whether he has an AI and an army of accomplices or not."

"I like your attitude, Erasmus. Stay in touch. I wondered how long we'd be without Ankh. Now is a critical time in the chase. This is when he would be most prone to making a mistake. At least he's in the open, especially if he is continuing to target alien diplomats. Is he trying to foment a revolution?" Rivka shook her head as she started to pace. "Remember the shooter's final words? Collum Gate had lost its way, but now the people have a chance for redemption, free from external influence."

Harpeth started to raise his hand as if requesting permission to speak. Rivka tipped her chin toward him.

"With his position at the *Collum Daily*, he could have planted a headline story that hits all the outlets declaring who knows what. Maybe their goal was nothing less than a civil war, trying to unite the people against the aliens."

"Erasmus?" Rivka requested.

"I am looking through the *Daily*'s servers now for pre-loaded stories. There is nothing in the queue, but he could have stored it off-site, like at the server farm. I'm running a worm to look for a time-activated program."

"Maybe we can just shut down the *Daily* in entirety. Cut all the feeds," Harpeth suggested.

"That might be exactly what he wants. That would be almost as telling as getting an official story that was misleading."

"If there are any new personals or new ads that are scheduled to start, replace all of them. We don't need him hiding his message in plain sight, either," Rivka directed.

After a few moments, Erasmus spoke. "That's done. I've also found a series of articles that were scheduled to run. One already has. I've removed it, and all references to it. Here it is for your review. At the bottom, you'll scroll into the other articles with the timestamps of when they were programmed to promulgate."

The first message was short, barely a paragraph, but it planted the seed for the stories that followed. Rivka read it out loud.

"Breaking News! A threat against the general population has been made. Law enforcement authorities have confirmed that it came from the alien sector, implying a purge of the human blight. The purveyor of the message remains on the loose and *Collum Daily*'s sources suggest the alien is under diplomatic immunity. We will share more when we know more."

"*That* won't incite the public," Supra Harpeth stated, sarcasm dripping from his words.

"I've already removed the article from the *Breaking News* feed. It is being buried to obscurity. The follow-up articles have all been quarantined."

"As soon as he realizes the other articles aren't being shown, he'll do one of two things: go to ground, as in disappear, or come out swinging like there's no tomorrow, because in his world, there won't be. What do you think?"

"I hope he mans up so I can punch his face and then toss his limp body to you for judgment," Red proclaimed. Lindy nodded in agreement.

"I think he will explode whatever bombs he has planted. Go out with a bang, and then go underground to drive the revolution manually," Erasmus offered.

"There won't be any revolution. No civil war, no war against aliens. We need to find this guy and put him down."

The supra's face turned hard. He was worn out from riding the day's emotional wave, and the real Harpeth was showing through. He had no patience for criminals. He didn't care whether they were aliens or humans, only that no one made trouble.

Rivka could sympathize. That was all she wanted, too.

"We'd better put together our response teams. Which target do we want him to go after?" Rivka asked.

"From a tactical standpoint, the Yollin compound is the most secure. The Ixtalis are self-contained. The Alaxar Trinary is what we call a soft target. Their compound is an open garden where people can commune with nature. And you know what the Crenellians have."

"They're the only ones outside an alien zone. That's

where he'll go," Rivka declared. "We've already been there. He'll hope that we've designated it secure and moved on. He failed to destroy it once. Maybe that is the challenge to his manhood I had hoped for. And the Crenellians are assholes."

Rivka turned and found Ankh sitting up and staring at her.

Jay glared through sleepy eyes.

"I meant *those* assholes, not you," Rivka clarified. Ankh's expression didn't change. "Supra Harpeth, bring your people together. I need to brief them on what's happening next."

CHAPTER EIGHTEEN

Thirty uniformed officers crowded a briefing room that was designed to comfortably handle a dozen. Red and Lindy stood outside the door to make more room. Ankh stood next to Rivka and was driving the video display.

"Listen up!" Harpeth bellowed. The room quieted. "The Magistrate is going to brief you on tonight's operation."

A simple introduction, but it was all Rivka needed. She nodded and tried to speak from her diaphragm to project her voice over the crowd. The first image Ankh showed was of the short message, the one Shnobhauer had planted.

"That was how it all started, but it wasn't really. It started a long time ago when a small group of people looked at the alien diplomats as the root cause of all the problems on Collum Gate. I exaggerate, but that is what the evidence seems to point to. At least two individuals were involved in this conspiracy and the murders that resulted from it. We have information that suggests he may attempt to bomb one or more of the following places."

Ankh dutifully showed pictures of the three embassies and Crenellations, Inc.

"My gut tells me that he'll go after the Crenellians again. He was stymied once, and I believe that his ego demands a rematch."

A few of the officers nodded. Others just took in the information. Most wore the blank expression of someone who had worked too many hours in a day.

Rivka needed their engagement. "Supra, please show them where they'll set up."

Ankh dutifully brought up diagrams of the buildings and the surrounding areas. Harpeth went through them one by one, designating teams of two and where they would be positioned. He kept five teams in reserve.

A specialist broke into the meeting and rushed to the front. She handed the supra a tablet and waited while he read it. When he was finished, she took it and left the room. Rivka looked at him expectantly.

When he finally decided to speak, it was in a low voice. "Shnobhauer has been spotted. My compliments to the Magistrate on making a positive impression on Crenellation, Inc's neighbors. Someone reported seeing our suspect—right before the Crenellians let him into their building."

Supra Harpeth put a hand on Ankh's shoulder and mumbled an apology. Ankh looked at the offending hand until the supra removed it.

"How can we get inside Crenellations, Inc?" Rivka asked.

"You can't. They have to let you in."

"Ankh! Did you say we can't?"

"Let me correct my statement. Crenellations, Inc is a fortress. It will be problematic to breach the defenses."

"What defenses?"

"Spring guns, lethal radiation barriers, gas clouds, and more auto-targeted weaponry."

"They didn't get approval for any of that!" Harpeth blurted.

"You can charge them if they survive." Rivka bent down to Ankh's level. "Is the Crenellian ambassador ready to make an appearance?"

"What could I do by getting inside?"

"What could *we* do, you mean?" Rivka pointed to herself. "You must have your bodyguard with you."

"No!" Red roared from the doorway. "Let *me* go. I look like a bodyguard. You look like the Magistrate."

Someone snickered.

Rivka wrestled with the decision. Red wasn't wrong, as was often the case.

"Ankh?"

"They will have physical barriers and technology to jam any signals into or out of the building," Ankh said in his usual emotionless voice.

"Well then, you and Red are going to have your work cut out for you. Bring him down and stop the attack. But you have to capture him alive because I need to talk to him."

"I don't think they'll let Vered in," Ankh said softly.

"You go in together or not at all."

"What's the contingency plan, Magistrate?" Harpeth asked.

"We go in heavy. Explosives and railguns to breach the

front door. We go in straight. The building is a fortress, right? Let's use that to not kill the hostages. I'm assuming there are hostages. What else would he be doing in there?"

Ankh's normally emotionless veneer slipped.

"He may be brokering a deal for more weapons."

"What the hell would the Crenellians do that for? They have to know we're looking for this guy!" Rivka's fists were jammed into her sides. She wasn't angry at Ankh. They had called him a traitor—the people who might be selling arms to a terrorist.

"It's what they do. They sell weapons," Ankh explained. "Crenellia is a planet on the frontier and is not yet a signatory to the Federation, although negotiations are ongoing."

"They won't fight once we're inside?"

"They will use their technology. If they are being held hostage, then Shnobhauer will use Crenellian technology. No matter who is in charge inside, you will have to fight the automated weaponry. If I'm inside when the systems are not actively engaged, Erasmus and I can probably access them and shut them off."

Rivka removed her datapad from the inside pocket of her Magistrate's jacket. She shivered, even though the room was hot. "Chaz, send a message to Crenellations, Inc that the Crenellian ambassador is on his way."

"I'll take five teams," Harpeth told the officers. He pointed at individuals, and they nodded to acknowledge. "The rest of you are on standby. Wait in the tactical deployment area two blocks from the target structure."

Rivka led the way out. When Ankh left the room, Red handed his railgun to Lindy and picked up the Crenellian. "You and me, buddy. Let's rock that guy's world."

"You can't kill him."

"You know I want to, Ankh, but I won't. The Magistrate will extract every bit of intel from his brain before judging him. My guess is that he'll die ugly."

"I think we all die ugly when it's time," Ankh replied.

"Damn. You two are bringing me down. I'd say don't take risks, but that would be abjectly moronic. Try to take risks that aren't too risky." Rivka wasn't sure she should hug Red since she didn't want to crush Ankh. In the end, she decided a gentle hand on Ankh's head would suffice. "Don't you dare die. Either of you. I should be the one going in there."

"The difference between you and us, Magistrate, is that we're expendable."

"I'm not," Ankh interjected.

Rivka snorted. "And neither are you, you big goon. I've gotten used to you blocking my sun. Don't make me try to find someone else. Lindy might miss you, too."

"Maybe," Lindy added.

Jay had been suspiciously absent from the conversation, so it surprised the others when she finally spoke. "I should go with them as Ankh's special assistant."

Red shook his head.

"I'd like that," Ankh said. Red stopped and stared.

"Say what?"

"Okay," Rivka found herself saying. The banter stopped as they climbed into the law enforcement van.

Ankh started his own briefing for Red and Jay. "My people are no physical threat to you, but under no circumstances should you allow them to touch or interact with any equipment..." He continued to talk until they arrived at the corner. They'd walk from there.

Rivka grimaced as the three exited the van. Red removed his vest and patted himself down. Rivka handed her neutron pulse weapon to him. It looked like a flashlight. He winked when he palmed it. Jay took Ankh's hand, and together they walked into the roadway and toward Crenellations, Inc.

Lindy stood shoulder to shoulder with the Magistrate.

"I feel like shit," Rivka stated.

"Me, too," Lindy agreed.

Harpeth sat in the passenger's seat, watching. "What now, Magistrate?"

"We prepare ourselves for a violent breach. Bring your explosives team and be ready."

Harpeth snapped his fingers, and two pairs of individuals jogged up. "Prepare for an explosive breach of the front door. On my order."

Lindy handed Red's railgun to Rivka. "For when the power of the law is secondary to physics."

"Blazer. I can't believe he named his gun."

"That's not the only gun he's named," Lindy hinted.

Rivka turned to her new teammate. "I'm glad you joined us. I'm sorry you have to be here for this. *I* don't even want to watch this. I like being on the doing end of things."

"I'm not sure I could be anywhere else right now, Magistrate." Lindy raised her railgun and tapped Blazer. "May this be resolved quickly. To the pain."

"To the pain," Rivka replied before chuckling. "Maybe we *should* have brought the mech."

We're walking toward the front door, Red reported over their internal comm link. He scanned the front of the building looking for weaponry, but nothing stuck out. He identified panels disguised to look like part of the building. *Emplacements. Good field of fire. Safe at the entrance.*

Roger, Rivka replied, unsure what Red's running narrative meant, but happy that he was engaged.

Jay pressed the button while Ankh stared at the camera. Red was surprised to hear it buzzing through the door. The deactivation had only been while he and Rivka were out front.

A Crenellian face appeared on the screen.

Probably not hostages. A Crenellian answered the doorbell, he relayed.

"What do you want?" the voice asked evenly.

"You know what I want," Ankh replied in the same tone.

"Maybe you can enlighten us, traitor."

"This could have gone one of two ways. I had hoped for the first while knowing the second was correct. Give up the human. He has crimes to answer for. And so, it appears, do you."

"We provide a valuable service to the entire galaxy."

"Of course, you do, but you don't need to supply terrorists. There are a great number of planets that could use Crenellian help, but your arrogance and egos are getting in the way of good business and technological advancement. There is more you don't know than you can imagine." Ankh stared emotionlessly at the screen.

Red nodded in appreciation of the monumental burn delivered by the tiny big-headed alien to his countrymen.

"You're not coming in," the Crenellian on the screen replied.

"I expected as much."

The screen went blank, and the door popped open. Ankh motioned for Red to enter. He hurried around Ankh and Jay and pushed the door open carefully as his eyes darted around the unknown entry. No one was there. He tiptoed through.

Ankh has opened the door. Follow us in, Red reported. *Erasmus?*

There is so much they don't know. Ankh's internal voice laughed. *By answering our ring, they opened the door and didn't even know it.*

"*Go, go, go!*" Rivka called as she and Lindy started running.

Harpeth was caught flat-footed. "Go where?"

"We're in," Rivka shouted over her shoulder as she turned the corner and ran toward Crenellations, Inc.

Ankh and Jay followed Red inside.

Goggles, the Crenellian told them before he moved his into place.

The lights went out. Emergency systems instantly appeared, bathing the area in red, but only for a few moments before they, too, disappeared.

Vered walked slowly as music started playing. Grainger's death metal. It wasn't loud, but it would cover any sound they made short of firing a railgun.

They'd become the predators. Red snarled, wishing for his railgun, when someone bumped into him from behind.

He glanced over his shoulder, where Rivka was holding Blazer out. He took it in one hand, passing the neutron pulse device to her with the other. He smiled savagely, his goggles hiding the determination in his eyes.

Lindy flared to his side, pointing to her goggles and then to the room on her right. She held up a single digit, drew a line across her throat, and stabbed a finger in the opposite direction. Red hatcheted his arm to the left and started moving that way.

I have a Crenellian at a workstation in front of me. He is working the keyboard. Lindy reported.

Shoot the computer, Ankh ordered.

She aimed and fired a single projectile. The railgun's crash shook the tables within the room, exploding the computer and blowing the Crenellian backward off his chair.

Oops, Lindy exclaimed. She moved carefully through the room toward the injured alien. Dropping to a knee, she kept her railgun pointed at a second doorway. The Crenellian's small neck pulsed with life. Lindy removed a zip tie from her pocket and locked his small arms behind his back.

Ankh strolled in behind her, stepping casually around the injured Crenellian.

What is this place? Jay asked.

A workshop. Look for a technology demonstration room, an immersive holographic experience. It helps sell the products when the buyers are on the receiving end of what the weapons can do. There may even be a live-fire system in the basement. I believe that's where the others will be.

There's no place to relax in here, Jay commented.

That's not what we do. There will be a nice kitchen and a

nice bathroom with a sauna. Engaging our minds is the epitome of who we are.

Are the weapons turned off, Ankh? We're not going to get lit up every time we walk into a room, are we? Rivka asked.

The systems are completely under Erasmus' control. If there is a standalone system, not on the grid, Erasmus cannot be held responsible for that. Ankh stopped and looked around. Jay kneeled next to him.

If there were such a system, Erasmus better tell us where it is, or he is responsible. Rivka was adamant about that. The more hope she had for getting through this without getting hurt, the more she wanted to come through unscathed.

She'd already shared some of her blood with the ground of Collum Gate. She wished to share no more of hers or from anyone on her team's.

Red and Rivka prowled through the left-hand rooms, which were austere and utilitarian, containing nothing of note. They reminded her of Ankh's cabin on *Peacekeeper*.

They need some color in their lives, she suggested.

We're at the door to the basement, Lindy relayed. Grainger's death metal continued to scrape across their eardrums. No one complained.

Wait there until we've checked upstairs, Rivka ordered.

Red and Rivka circled back to the front of the building and slowly climbed the curving staircase. A marble railing arced upward, drawing the eye to a skylight above, currently filled with the dark of the night sky. Whoever built it took care with the simple elegance. Rivka appreciated the beauty in the single moment she allowed herself.

Red quickly moved off the steps and onto the balcony. He stopped to survey his surroundings, crouching to make himself a smaller target. Rivka ducked behind him, understanding why but thinking it did little for a man of Red's size. He waved at her to follow, and they started at the far end to funnel anyone who ran down the stairs and out the front door to where Harpeth and his men should be.

The farthest room was the sleeping quarters. Six small beds were arrayed in two rows. More physical austerity from the cerebral race.

Room after room, labs and workshops, but the last room they checked, the one closest to the staircase, was the largest and completely packed with military hardware. There was even a satellite hanging from the ceiling. A plasma weapon's launch barrel protruded from it, pointing directly at the door through which they'd entered.

Once Red confirmed that no one was hiding in the display room he whispered, "How'd they get this stuff up here?"

Rivka shrugged. None of the equipment was manned. It was all made to be operated remotely. Effortless warfare.

"I'm glad Ankh is on our side, but I'm not liking his people much."

"The galaxy will be fine without this crap. War needs to be expensive; have a high cost in lives, so people think twice before waging it."

They're coming out, Lindy blurted directly into their minds.

In a rush, the door popped open, and a small bot ran headlong into Lindy. She had been ready but still wasn't able to respond before being bowled over backward. The suspect was next out, delivering a stiff arm to Jay's forehead before running for the front door. Four Crenellians rushed out and tried to grab Ankh.

Jay picked him up and spun, delivering a back kick that impacted the chest of the closest Crenellian. She spun back, throwing a wild roundhouse kick at the other four. They dodged back, one of them tripping over their prone comrade.

With Ankh still in her arms. Jay closed on them. "Leave him alone!" she shouted. The Crenellians backed away as she kicked at their faces.

Maybe you should make them lie on the floor? Ankh suggested.

"Get on the floor! On your faces, maggots!" Jay was unhappy. Not only had she been attacked, but she was also afraid she'd killed one of the Crenellians. He was on the floor, unmoving, unblinking eyes staring at nothing.

The others assumed the face-down position, and Jay started to hyperventilate.

He's running toward the front door! Lindy passed.

We're upstairs, Rivka replied. She and Red bolted from the room and jumped down the stairs, hitting the fifth step down, before leaping again. The suspect appeared for a moment as he ran through the foyer and into the entryway. Bodies collided with grunts.

"Got you," Harpeth declared. "Cuff him and hold him tight."

Rivka and Red hit the bottom step together, finally slowing when they saw the uniformed personnel blocking the entryway. They held a struggling and squirming figure.

"Please turn the lights on, Erasmus," Rivka requested. The lights blazed to life, bathing the area in their warm glow.

One of the officers grabbed a handful of hair and turned the man's face toward Rivka.

"Bindola Shnobhauer. At last, we meet," she said coldly, watching Harpeth to see if he would take the man away before she could talk to him. Zombie him.

CHAPTER NINETEEN

She grabbed him by the arm and looked into his dark eyes, the depths of which seemed empty. The spark of life and joy was gone. She could feel the despair within his mind.

"Who else is killing the aliens?" she demanded. No one. The shooter had been a pleasant surprise, a competent marksman to join the cause of Collum First. She saw in Bindola's mind the knife attack that he'd made on the ambassador. It had given him a feeling of superiority for a few moments. It had given him joy.

Rivka let go and stepped away.

"What'd you see?" Harpeth asked.

"He is a very sick man. His mind is genius, and his rational being is almost gone. He's to be pitied. Supra, find everyone associated with Collum First. You'll want to talk to them about their irrational hatred toward aliens."

Rivka moved close to grip Shnobhauer by the neck. "Where were you going in such a hurry?"

Away. Anywhere but there.

"Where is your bomb factory?"

Factory? Each one is a work of art. A bomb studio...yes. That's what it is.

"You'll want to bring the Crenellians in, too. He was making bombs in the basement. He attached one of those bombs to our van to destroy the evidence and his accomplices," Rivka told the supra. "No honor among this band of thieves."

Supra Harpeth waved his officers past. Lindy was in the doorway, waiting while Jay hovered over the prone captives, unable to take her eyes from the alien she'd killed.

"One last question," Rivka started. "You worked with aliens to kill aliens. How do you justify that within that brain of yours?"

Fury! The aliens are all predators. Turn them against each other. They are nothing more than genetic failures on a galactic scale.

"Indeed," Rivka replied. "Lock him up forever. He's taken his last breath of free air. For the record, Bindola Shnobhauer, you have been judged."

Harpeth nodded before shaking his head. "You know our laws, Magistrate. He'll be executed before the night is out."

"Why? What will capital punishment do in this case?"

The supra looked around before leaning close and speaking in a hush. "Because we have to win, and win big. No one can rise from the penal system and challenge authority. Not someone with his disdain for life."

"There's no cost savings?"

"Of course there is. We'd pay for rehabilitation if it worked, but the recidivism rate is too high. None of the training or touchy-feely programs work with any semblance of reliability."

"So you make the problem go away?" Rivka cocked her head to give him side-eye.

"We deal with such problems in a definitive way." Harpeth didn't invite further discussion on the subject as Bindola Shnobhauer was shackled and led to a waiting cruiser. He was chained to a ring inside the vehicle, and two officers took positions on either side of him. With a lead and trail car, the small convoy lifted into the air and raced away.

Four Crenellians appeared in handcuffs. The fifth required a stretcher, and the sixth needed a body bag. They were sequestered while waiting for a vehicle to take them away.

Rivka and Red joined the others in the back where steps led to the basement. Ankh was trying to guide Jay from the building, but she wouldn't budge. She continued to stare at the spot on the floor where the dead Crenellian had lain. Rivka was torn between wanting to look in the basement and helping her crew.

Red saved her from having to make the decision. "Lindy and I will take a look downstairs. Watch over them while we're gone." Red pointed with his chin at Ankh and Jay.

"Will do, Boss," Rivka replied. The big man nodded, and together with Lindy, they headed below ground. Five minutes later, they returned. "Too many weapons and explosives. I'm surprised they didn't blow themselves up."

"Anything else?"

"Computer systems. A bunch of them; probably run all the different toys they have in this place. I'm not sure how you would dismantle a weapons cache like we have here. If you blew it in place, secondary explosions would level the block."

"We'll leave that for Harpeth to figure out. Jay, honey? Come with us. I think we'll go back to our ship now and get some rest."

Law enforcement vehicles were stacked up in front of Crenellations, Inc. The ambulance pulled up and removed the injured alien. Two officers climbed into the back with him. The body bag went into a different vehicle. The four prisoners were put in the back of a windowless hover sedan. Ankh stood tall on the steps as he watched his people hauled away.

When Crenellations, Inc was cleared, Supra Harpeth posted guards and attached a special magnetic lock to the front door. "What do you say we look this place over when we have fresh minds?" Harpeth asked.

"What do you say we turn this over to the Federation? R2D2 will be interested in taking this place apart."

"What's an Arty Deetoo?" the supra asked.

"The Federation's research and development team. I don't know who else could dismantle that place without destroying everything on this block."

"I'd like to collect evidence to support the charges I'm going to file against the Crenellians." Harpeth wasn't playing. Rivka knew that their support of the terrorist made them guilty as if they had planted the bombs themselves.

"We're going to let the Federation retain custody of them. And actually, as soon as possible, I'll take them with me. I expect that I'll be sent to Crenellia anyway in order to talk about this and the Crenellian role in the galaxy. If their involvement were to become common knowledge, they would become pariahs. They can serve a purpose, but not in the weapons bazaar."

"I'd like to prosecute them, Magistrate." Harpeth crossed his arms and clenched his jaw.

"Of course, you would. Things have been going so well, Supra. I'd hate to see that spoiled. Deal with Shnobhauer as you wish, but have the Crenellians meet me at my ship as soon as possible. Bring the dead one and the broken one, too. We'll take them home in disgrace."

Harpeth huffed once before nodding. "As you wish." He waited for the Magistrate and her people to board the law enforcement van and move away before he left the crime scene. Two cars and four officers were on guard, and would remain on guard until the Federation relieved them.

The city's lights sparkled, a welcoming visual treat for anyone who took the time to look. When the city's inhabitants awoke the next morning, they'd go about their lives, never knowing what cesspool had lurked beneath. The alien population would know about the capture of the perp, although it would be a while before they returned to openly moving about within the city.

Fear had been planted, and like a mighty oak, it would remain steadfast against the winds of change.

"First one is always the hardest. I'll never forget mine," Red said, trying to console Jayita.

"Nor mine," Lindy added. Hers was far more recent, but she had been as prepared for it as one could be.

"But the difference between yours and everyone else's is that yours was self-defense. What would they have done if they had gotten to Ankh? Evil people do evil things, and it takes good people doing bad things to stop them. It may not make you feel any better right now, but that's what our line of work is all about. We're not here to coddle those who have lost their way. Ours is to kick their asses so hard they never see the light of day again. Sometimes it hurts us as much as it hurts them. May we never stop caring so much that it doesn't hurt."

Rivka poured a round of drinks for the four of them. Ankh didn't drink, but he didn't leave while they did.

"Here's to keeping the peace." Rivka clinked the glass in Jay's hand.

The young woman finally looked up. She studied the faces of the four people around her. Determination. Justice. Freedom. The law. "I guess I could have worse company," Jay quipped.

"You gave me the finger!" Rivka smiled.

"And you damn near ripped that finger off."

"Damn straight." Rivka threw back her shot and held out the glass for a second round.

"I'm sorry to interrupt, Magistrate, but law enforcement has arrived with the Crenellian prisoners."

"Ankh? Are you okay with us transporting them to Crenellia?"

"Yes. Why wouldn't I be?" Ankh asked innocently.

"Because they called you a traitor and said you were shunned."

"Did you believe that?"

Rivka met Ankh's unblinking gaze. "Not in the least."

"Then what's the problem?"

"Chaz, open the door and let's bring them aboard," Rivka requested.

Lindy took Red's railgun and headed for the cabinet they considered to be their armory. She locked the weapons inside while Red cracked his knuckles and looked intimidating. The four uninjured Crenellians carried the body bag containing their dead compatriot. The fifth alien limped heavily, using a cane to keep from falling over. Rivka made them put the body by the main hatch before they shuffled to the rec room.

"Sit here," she ordered them. Because of their shackles, they were unable to climb into the human-sized chairs. "On the floor, then. It's padded." Once in place, they sat rigidly, unmoving and not making eye contact.

Ankh sauntered in. He looked at the chair that loomed over his fellows. Rivka picked him up and set him in place.

"It is not Crenellia's place to arm terrorists and cause civil wars. I was in one, and only later did I see the terrible cost that was on my head, on our heads. You should be ashamed of yourselves." Ankh's voice was even, but a vein began to throb in his skinny neck.

"Who should be ashamed?"

Rivka couldn't tell which of the five had spoken. They didn't move their mouths much when they talked.

"Enough!" Rivka told them. "Prisoners don't have the

right to speak on board my ship." She glared at them until she was sure they weren't going to talk again.

Hamlet appeared in the corridor and stretched, showing his claws and fangs before sauntering toward the aliens. He rubbed his face on one, and then the next. They shied away from the cat as if he were poisonous. He didn't care.

He was a cat. The more they tried to lean away, the more he wanted to climb on them. After he had tormented them all, Jay scooped him up and headed toward her cabin. Lindy and Red took seats in the recliners. "We'll watch them, Magistrate. I expect you have a report to write."

"I do." Rivka moved toward the bridge. "Chaz, take us to Crenellia, best possible speed."

Peacekeeper remained on station according to the instructions from Crenellian traffic control. The armaments and defensive systems between the planet and orbit were more than Rivka wanted to tangle with. It was a technological demonstration and a visible portfolio for any buyers with deep pockets.

Four hours they waited. Rivka had fallen asleep when Chaz alerted her. "We're being guided in, Magistrate on a one-time-use travel corridor. They warn us not to stray from the designated path or risk instant destruction."

"Then don't stray." Rivka yawned.

"I shan't," Chaz confirmed. The ship spiraled downward until it descended onto a remote parking apron on the far side of the spaceport. After it landed, they waited.

"Do you think they'll send a car?" Rivka asked aloud, not expecting an answer.

"We could just kick them out and go," Red suggested.

"That's not a bad idea." Rivka scratched her chin, wondering if the prisoners were uncomfortable. They'd been on the floor for a long time.

"That's a horrible idea!" Lindy stood, giving Red a dirty look. "They're in our care, so we have to take care of them."

"They'll be taken care of. I'll be with them."

Red jumped up and ran to the weapons locker. He hauled out the railguns and handheld weapons. He and Lindy armored up and prepared to go.

"We may not need the full package." Rivka pointed to herself and her usual Magistrate garb.

"Maybe we take the mech this time?"

"I have no intention of making you or this ship an impact crater because we incited the Crenellians. I wonder how many weapons they have pointed at us right now?"

"All of them?" Ankh ventured.

"Maybe you should stay with the ship."

Ankh looked at her as he usually did. She couldn't tell if he was confused, belligerent, or simply questioning her statement.

"Fine. You can come."

"Is Crenellia a signatory of the Federation?"

"Not yet," Rivka said slowly.

"Then what the hell are we doing here? What if they try to arrest us? I'm not getting hauled off to prison by a mob of tiny big-heads."

"Since the Federation is in active negotiations with Crenellia, we *do* have recognized diplomatic status. Don't worry, Gulliver, I won't let them haul you away." She kneeled in the middle of the sitting group. "Get up. It's time to go."

Red mashed the button, and the hatch opened. Temperatures were mild. Rivka waited for the group to pick up the body bag and shuffle out. Rivka looked behind her, expecting to see Ankh. Jay was there, holding his hand. She looked curiously at the body bag.

"Terrorists have a way of ending up dead," Lindy said pleasantly, slapping Jay on the back. "Fuck those guys."

Jay smirked, her eyebrows furrowed.

Lindy shrugged. "It's how I feel. What do you say we dump this trash and go home? I'm ready for some private time with my man."

Jay blinked quickly, and Lindy winked at her.

"Damn." Rivka motioned for everyone to keep moving. She felt like she was chaperoning a third-grade class to the aquarium.

Before they hit the bottom of the stairs, a shuttle flew in and landed not far from *Peacekeeper*'s stubby wing. First off was a human wearing a Federation pin.

"I'm Hans Sedolin, assistant to the lead negotiator." The young man smiled broadly, nodding to Rivka and her group. "I'm sorry you had to wait. Getting clearance to go anywhere takes forever. You'd think the Crenellians would be more efficient, but sometimes they have to put the aliens in their place. Well, all the time, actually. No matter. We are at their main government building where their ruling council resides. That's where these five are supposed to go. Climb aboard, and let's see if we can make record time getting back."

"Nice to meet you, Hans. I'm Magistrate Rivka Anoa. That's Red, Lindy, Jay, and Ankh'Po'Turn. These are the ones who were running Crenellations, Inc. We're giving them back to their government. If we'd left them on Collum Gate they would have been executed, so here we are."

He ushered them onto the cramped shuttle. Rivka made the Crenellians stand while her team took the seats. Hans was granted immediate clearance, and he wasted no time taking off and zooming toward the city.

They're starting to get nervous, Ankh told Rivka's team.

How can you tell? Red wondered. Ankh gave him his best blank stare.

Are you thinking that their little operation on Collum Gate was unsanctioned? Relief washed over Rivka like spring rain. *I thought we were going to have to fight your entire race.*

Yes and no, Ankh replied.

Yes and no what?

Yes, I believe they were acting independently, and no, you won't have to fight all Crenellians.

The shuttle approached a building that would be described as a megalith on any other planet—a monstrous structure with multiple landing pads dotting the rooftop. It was a massive rectangle, all black, windows indistinguishable from the structure. Hans landed the shuttle without the slightest bump and dropped the ramp. Red was first out, scanning the rooftop and neighboring landing pads for threats.

The building had turrets with weapons' barrels protruding. Automated weapons systems—a Crenellian favorite.

Rivka joined Red.

"What do you think?"

"I think I'm ready for this one to be over, Magistrate."

"We're on the final leg. We'll drag our carcasses over the finish line and collapse on the other side. But we've already won. No more diplomats died after our arrival." The main government building dominated the landscape. The entire city spread before them—a great view with nothing to see. "A little color wouldn't hurt anyone."

Hans led the way, going slowly so the shackled Crenellians carrying the bag could keep up.

No one offered them a hand. *You made your bed, now lie in it,* they thought.

Once inside, they were met by an older human and a group of five Crenellians.

Rivka hurried forward and offered her hand. "General Reynolds, what are you doing out here?"

"I could ask you the same thing, Magistrate," the General replied, smiling easily. "These fine folks are the Crenellian Leadership Council. They're in charge of all things Crenellia. They were very interested to hear the story you told and voila! Here you are body-slamming this pack of scumbags. They'll take them from here."

One of the council tapped on a datapad, and a series of bots streamed forward. Each collected one of the prisoners, securing the shackles to a pad on which the prisoner stood. The bots flowed away.

"They didn't plead for their lives," Jay blurted.

"Jayita." Lance Reynolds waved to her.

"They wouldn't," Ankh explained. "It is not our way. They were caught. They will be punished."

"Does Crenellia have executions?"

"Of course not. That is barbaric. I thank you on behalf of my people for not letting them remain on Collum Gate where they would have been put to death. Our punishments are much worse. We have remote outposts." Ankh's whole body shook in the way his people did when they laughed.

Rivka thought he was having a seizure every time she saw it.

The council stepped forward and spoke as one. "We welcome the Federation's assistance in finding these criminals and helping us bring them to justice. We hope that we can return the favor someday. And to you, Ankh'Po'Turn, you are welcome on Crenellia any day as a favored son who has faithfully carried the banner of our people into the bosom of the greatest power since the Kurtherians."

"Join the Federation and help us help others," Lance stated.

I'm sure the main sticking point in the negotiations is the arms trade, Rivka asserted.

Alas, 'tis true. It's their main export and their primary source of revenue. We can't cover the shortfall, so we have to figure out how the arms trade can work within the Federation's legal framework. It's somewhat of a shitshow.

Somewhat, *General?*

He laughed. *It's a total shitshow, but Rome wasn't built in a day. Can you stay and help me with some of the legalese?*

"Oh," Rivka blurted aloud.

The General laughed even harder. "I'm kidding. Take your team home and get some R&R. That's an order, Magistrate."

"Yes, sir. You heard him, people. Saddle up!"

Rivka hugged the man who was the nominal head of the Federation, hundreds of planets strong and growing every day. She was one small piece in the big puzzle. So many teams like hers, overt and covert, risked their lives to keep the peace.

"Thanks, Rivka. And thank you all." The General nodded and motioned for the council to lead on.

Rivka twirled her finger in the air. "Time to go home."

CHAPTER TWENTY

"I still have that bitch's shirt!" Rivka said from her cabin.

"I'd like to see the law that says you can take the shirt from someone who caused your shirt to get ruined." Red raised an eyebrow at his boss.

"That was an on-the-spot civil claim for damages. It was properly adjudicated," Rivka held her head up as she made her proclamation.

"I'm sure it was. What's on the docket next?"

"Take some time off, Red. Don't go too far, because as soon as I can get a lead on one of your former employers, we're leaving to go set things straight."

Lindy and Red locked fingers.

"I made reservations at the honeymoon suite at the top of the station. It boasts a panoramic view of the stars."

"Don't you have to get married to be newlyweds?" Rivka looked from one face to the next. Red shrugged.

"Magistrates can marry people, can't they?"

"Magistrates, boat captains, and concerned citizens

who paid their money and took an online course—like a particular dentist we all know."

"We're not getting married by a dentist!" Lindy declared.

"Aha! You are getting married." Rivka threw the bitch's shirt on the floor and stepped on it on her way to hug Lindy and Red.

"What do you say we skip the formalities and head straight to the honeymoon suite?" Red wondered, running a hand slowly over his bald head.

"Sounds good. See you when we see you." The lovebirds hurried away before anyone could change their mind.

Ankh was in his lab working on a new piece of hardware. His night-vision goggles remained a fixture on his forehead. Jay sat by herself in the rec room with Hamlet in her lap. She absentmindedly stroked his fur to rhythmic purring.

"How are you doing, Jay?"

"Just killing time before my shift."

"What are you talking about?"

"I work at the spa now. Evening clerk and general cleaning."

"Do they know your hours aren't going to be regular or even predictable? I need you with me. You're a valuable member of our team."

"I know all that, and I thank you for your kind words and hospitality. But I really like the spa, and by working there, if there is an opening, I can snag the time for almost nothing. I get paid and pay off my debt that much sooner. It's a win-win."

The End

Serial Killer - Judge, Jury, & Executioner, Book 3
If you like this book, please leave a review. This is a new series, so the only way I can decide whether to commit more time to it is by getting feedback from you, the readers. Your opinion matters to me. Continue or not? I have only so much time to craft new stories. Help me invest that time wisely. Plus, reviews buoy my spirits and stoke the fires of creativity.

Don't stop now! Keep turning the pages as Craig & Michael talk about their thoughts on this book and the overall project called the Age of Expansion.

Your new favorite legal eagle will return!

AUTHOR NOTES - CRAIG MARTELLE

WRITTEN SEPTEMBER 1ST, 2018

You are still reading! Thank you so much. It doesn't get much better than that.

I think the Executioner series is my best-received series out of all of them that I've done. Thank you to you wonderful people for joining me. I really like this series, and enjoy writing it.

I'm getting a few questions regarding more backstory for some of the characters. We'll reveal little bits and pieces with each new book in this series. One of the main questions surrounds the Rangers-turned-Magistrates. I've talked to Michael extensively about this. He numbered each of the Rangers in *The Kurtherian Gambit*, but the universe is a big place and they needed more reach, so there are secondary Rangers—those brought on board by the main Rangers and sent to the outer reaches to do what Rangers do. They were of sound character, but still the second string.

It is from this group (and there were a great many Rangers who fell into the second string) that we find our Magistrates. Grainger, Jael, Chi, and Buster were grunts, saved by a werewolf (who happened to be a Ranger), and then moved into the Ranger ranks. As for which Ranger? We'll keep you guessing for now. Michael and the Just In Time readers are keeping me on my toes in regards to canon. We don't want anything to conflict with what we know from the KGU. I spent a couple hours on just a few sentences in order to get them right.

This book is the first time this group will have worked as a team since they were transformed into Rangers and then Magistrates.

So I went right to the top. Natalie Grey came up with a crossover piece so Barnabas could make an appearance, talk to the Magistrates, and make some magic happen. I am so happy to have that addition to this book. Thank you, and thanks to Michael, who gave it a read and two thumbs up.

I needed some DNA terminology, and from the UK, I found this site extremely helpful - http://aboutforensics. co.uk/dna-analysis/.

Once my dentist, Dr. Tyler Ingersoll, found out that I was writing this series, he offered the bit about genetic dental issues that I worked into the plot. I think it made for a great conclusion to the clone sub-plot while allowing me to discuss some other legal elements. I have to research a great deal with this series. I was able to wing a lot of stuff in the post-apocalyptic series, but I can't do that here.

What if someone was cloned? Can you exist without a birth certificate? Of course you can, but can you do anything more than just exist? What will the law allow? Interesting hypotheticals, to say the least, so I put my twist and stamp on them and then moved to the main event.

Murder!

- Recruits and Rookies - rank is Losta
- Patrol officers, the uniforms - Petro
- Patrol leaders, older, still in uniform – Hardco
- Detectives, Investigators (different uniform) – Stigo
- Specialists (bomb techs, forensics, etc.) - Specialist
- Investigation leaders (no uniform, but formal dress, like a suit) – Supra
- Police leadership (senior nonuniform ranks) - Guvna

I had an awful lot of help from people regarding names. Here's what I used and who I have to thank.

Tommy Donbavand – Parkilo Prime, populated by a sentient plant species and Nat Ferider.

Micky Cocker supplied a nice list of names, of which I picked - Y'eaton, Zaria,

Sc'allid, Harpeth, Opheramin, Collum Gate, and Jurdenia.

I hope everyone enjoyed this story. It was fun to write in a way that I found most relaxing. James Caplan, Micky Cocker, and Kelly O'Donnell keep me on the straight and narrow with in-process reads and ideas, language smoothing, continuity, and overall readability. They are an amazing bunch who help make me and my stories better.

No one goes on this journey alone. If it weren't for being surrounded by great people and the incredible readers who keep picking up my books, none of these stories would be possible.

Peace, fellow humans.

Please join my Newsletter (www.craigmartelle.com – please, please, please sign up!), or you can follow me on Facebook since you'll get the same opportunity to pick up the books for only 99 cents on that first day they are published.

If you liked this story, you might like some of my other books. You can join my mailing list by dropping by my website **www.craigmartelle.com** or if you have any comments, shoot me a note at craig@craigmartelle.com. I am always happy to hear from people who've read my work. I try to answer every email I receive.

If you liked the story, please write a short review for me on Amazon. I greatly appreciate any kind words; even one or two sentences go a long way. The number of reviews an ebook receives greatly improves how well an ebook does on Amazon.

Amazon – www.amazon.com/author/craigmartelle

BookBub – https://www.bookbub.com/authors/craig-martelle

Facebook – www.facebook.com/authorcraigmartelle

My web page – www.craigmartelle.com

That's it—break's over, back to writing the next book. Peace, fellow humans.

Author Notes – Michael Anderle
September 12, 2018
(a very special day to me)

P(re).S. – Thank you to our Beta Readers, JIT Team, Editing Team, and the Operations and Art folks who helped create this book. It is a P.S. that is so important, it goes first.

Are you reading this? Then I have a SPECIAL thank for to you. I turn fifty-one today. A bit of an accomplishment, and a sign I can't deceive myself any longer about the truth.

I am on the 'other side' of youth.

I'm in the maturing stage of life. It's time for me to put on that hat of wisdom and see into the future, providing insightful stories which cause readers to read and reread the book for nuggets which will illuminate the cosmos and bring peace and harmony to alien inter-species relationships throughout the galaxy.

Or, you know, I can write more stories where we blow

shit up, and hope the alien inter-species issue is solved by someone in the future.

I think I like that option more...

Imagination BECAME reality

I remember reading an article where scientist (of that time) admit to reading science-fiction and watching *Star Trek* and it made their minds explode with ideas. The concepts they believed were cool in their youth drove them to their work paths in the future, and still excited them in their day-to-day activities as they actually created the theories and working prototypes to bring what had only been imagination to fruition.

I have to admit I (one day) hope to create some cool piece of technology in a story which becomes a reality in the future.

I'm ready for the future of learning (very small rant from a fifty-one-year old – I'm becoming a curmudgeon I think... Just ignore this)

It is no great stretch to say that most adults who worry about education around the world believe we can do better. Now, "better" might require parents to get involved, which (if we have one-parent families trying to place food on the table) might require help from the community, etc., etc.

Or, you know, we the general populace of science-fiction readers might decide to band together and cobble together the technology and research of today and build an infrastructure of classes, training, testing, and laws (yes, we would have to change the laws, I think. At least in a lot of the states in the US. I can't speak to the laws in other countries.)

I bet we HAVE the core technology infrastructure right now to create the virtual school of tomorrow. I can imagine a way we get there from here, and it will have to deal with so much political crap it's crazy. For example, 2016 instructional spending (which is not total spending, just the instructional aspect) was $4,077 in Arizona and $15,746 in New York.

Scratching my chin (and being a bit cynical), I imagine New York might have some explaining to do on that high of a spend. My (admittedly very fast WIKI lookup) suggests that New York is 37 out of 50 in educational attainment (% High School Attainment levels)

(https://en.wikipedia.org/wiki/ List_of_U.S._states_by_educational_attainment)

I tend to be a "follow the money" sort of fellow. I believe New York probably suffers from challenges which Arizona does not.

So, how can we dream up a system which supports BOTH of these great states? We have free teaching already (just go online and check out videos from well-known universities.)

Often, it is not the teachers who are lacking, but the infrastructure (both material and immaterial) which is hampering both teachers and the operations group.

Or hell, they suck! (Which is a possibility.)

I suspect that in my lifetime we will have a completely new paradigm of teaching and I'd love it to be from Science-Fiction fans that made it happen. For an extensive discussion of one such system, check out *Crescendo of Fire*, (click here) the second book in LMBPN's Braintrust series by Marc Stiegler, and *Let the Bits Run Free*, also by Marc Stiegler, an educational short story which will be on LMBPN's Ear Crush Podcast Friday September 21st. (http://lmbpn.com/earcrush/).

There, I've added the necessary societal thoughts into the book, woven in delicately between the first page and the last.

So, anyone ready to go blow shit up and take out the bad guys?

Because I'm fifty-one, not dead.

Ad Aeternitatem,

Michael Anderle

BOOKS BY CRAIG MARTELLE

Craig Martelle's other books (listed by series)

Terry Henry Walton Chronicles (co-written with Michael Anderle) – a post-apocalyptic paranormal adventure

Gateway to the Universe (co-written with Justin Sloan & Michael Anderle) – this book transitions the characters from the Terry Henry Walton Chronicles to The Bad Company

The Bad Company (co-written with Michael Anderle) – a military science fiction space opera

End Times Alaska (also available in audio) – a Permuted Press publication – a post-apocalyptic survivalist adventure

The Free Trader – a Young Adult Science Fiction Action Adventure

Cygnus Space Opera – A Young Adult Space Opera (set in the Free Trader universe)

Darklanding (co-written with Scott Moon) – a Space Western

Judge, Jury, & Executioner – a space opera adventure legal thriller

Rick Banik – Spy & Terrorism Action Adventure

Become a Successful Indie Author – a non-fiction work

Metamorphosis Alpha – stories from the world's first science fiction RPG

The Expanding Universe – science fiction anthologies

Shadow Vanguard – a Tom Dublin series

Uprise Saga – an Amy DuBoff series

Enemy of my Enemy (co-written with Tim Marquitz) – A galactic alien military space opera

Superdreadnought (co-written with Tim Marquitz) – a military space opera (coming fall of 2018)

Made in the USA
Columbia, SC
03 March 2023